D0873911

INSTRUCTIONAL

IMc MEDIA
CENTER

C.W. POST CAMPUS OF L.I.U.

BOOKS BY VIOLET OLSEN

The Growing Season
Never Brought to Mind
View from the Pighouse Roof

View
From The
Pighouse
Roof

View From The Pighouse Roof

৯ৡ VIOLET OLSEN ৯ৡ

Atheneum   1987   New York

Atheneum
Macmillan Publishing Company
866 Third Avenue, New York, NY 10022

Composition by Arcata Graphics/Kingsport, Kingsport, Tennessee
Printed and bound by Arcata Graphics/Fairfield, Pennsylvania
Designed by Marjorie Zaum
First Edition

10 9 8 7 6 5 4 3 2 1

Library of Congress Cataloging-in-Publication Data

Olsen, Violet.
view from the pighouse roof.

SUMMARY: Twelve-year-old Marie, living with her widowed mother, brothers,
sisters on an Iowa farm
during the Depression, tries to cope with the difficulties of growing up.
[1. Depressions—1929—Fiction. 2. Farm life—Iowa—
Fiction. 3. Danish Americans—Fiction. 4. Family life—
Fiction] I. Title.
PZ7.051785Vi   1987   [Fic]   86–22223
ISBN 0–689–31324–1

For my grandchildren:

Rachael Clare
Ruth Ann
Christopher Canton
Jacob Benjamin
Alexis Hope
LaRae Margaret
Karla Jamie
Genevieve Elizabeth
Patrick William
Jacob Henry
Martha Jane
Margaret Erin

Author's Note

There comes a time when history turns a corner. An event happens and life can never go back to being as it was before. Such an event was the black Tuesday in October 1929 when the stock market crashed.

Within this web of complex circumstances, children were born and lived. Things beyond their control shaped and molded their lives. Yet these children grew and learned despite the Great Depression that marked the decade of the 1930s. They raised structures upon which the children of today and tomorrow will continue to build and create new structures.

All are architects of Fate
   Working in these Walls of Time
Some with massive deeds and great,
   Some with ornaments of rhyme.
Nothing useless is, or low,
   Each thing in its place is best
And what seems but idle show
   Strengthens and supports the rest.
For the structure that we raise,
   Time is with materials filled
Our to-days and yesterdays
   Are the blocks with which we build.

Henry Wadsworth Longfellow
1807–1882

Contents

CONTENTS

View
From The
Pighouse
Roof

❧ 1 ❧

Christmas Day 1933

"I DON'T CARE. I WON'T GO!"

Marie turned her face away from Mamma to hide the tears she felt filling her eyes. She was angry now and in no mood to talk to anybody, least of all Mamma!

"You can't stay home alone on Christmas day. Come now, Marie, put on your pretty red dress. We will wait for you to get dressed. You don't look so bad." Mamma put her hand on Marie's arm and Marie turned to face her mother, no longer bothering to hide the tears.

"No! I said I'm not going and I'm not. Just go! All of you! I want to stay home by myself."

"Marie, you should come with us. There's nothing good to eat here at home," said Karen coaxingly. "You'll be sorry after we leave and you start getting hungry."

Lars was standing by the kitchen door, wearing his cap

and overcoat, and Marie knew he was getting impatient. He had the keys to the Essex in his hand.

"Oh, let her stay home, Ma," Lars said. "All she ever thinks about is how she looks." Then he laughed. It was the crowning insult.

"She's right in a way," he continued. "She does look sick with all those cold sores puffing up her mouth and it would be pretty unappetizing for anybody sitting across from her at the dinner table. Her lower lip is so swollen and sticks out so far all she needs is a ring hanging from. . . ."

"Shut up, Lars," screamed Marie.

"Go start the car, Lars," ordered Mamma. "You stay home, Marie, if that's what you want. I'll have Katie fix a nice Christmas dinner plate and somebody will bring it to you. After all, we will just be across the road at the neighbors'. You go upstairs and go back to bed if you don't feel so well. Tomorrow you will feel better."

They left then and Marie was glad. Now that Mamma, Lars, and Karen had gone to the Tornquists' house to eat their Christmas dinner, she could release all the hot tears of self-pity that she'd tried to hold back. She could give vent to all the physical and emotional pain, the injustice, the outrage cold sores caused. She could really cry now! Nobody was around to poke fun at her. So Marie cried, and the hot sting of tears added to the discomfort of her swollen lips and made her feel worse.

It wasn't fair! She'd *wanted* to go to Katie's house for Christmas dinner. She *was* hungry and Katie Tornquist was one of the best cooks in the county. She often took first prize at the Clay County Fair for her baking. Marie always had fun playing checkers or cards with Norman and Lyle Tornquist, the neighbor boys she'd known ever since she started school.

It wasn't fair! Nobody else in the family ever got cold sores. At least not so terrible that they puffed their lips out like an inner tube. Marie sat with her head buried in her arms at the kitchen table. She felt the cold slick surface of the oilcloth, and was sure she would remember Christmas 1933, as one of the most miserable days of her life.

Marie remembered other Christmases when Alfred, Rosie, and Cora were home—when they had huge Christmas trees, decorated and lighted, with packages piled high, stockings hung, and sleigh rides. Relatives came and Cora played Christmas carols, everybody sang, and ate roast goose with all the trimmings. Those were the good Christmases before the Depression, when the whole family was together. Before Rosie and Alfred left home. Before Cora spent every minute she could with her boyfriend, Milton Hayes, and his family. Before she, Marie, started getting cold sores every time she got a sniffle. Marie finished up her crying jag with a few more sniffles and wondered if and when life would ever again be happy for her as it had been long ago before the Depression ruined everything for the whole family.

Karen was right. There was nothing good to eat here at home. No candy, fruit, or nuts. Last night, Christmas Eve, the whole family had gone to Tante Karen and Uncle Soren's farm for a big dinner. Mamma had said it was nice not to have to do holiday cooking and baking for a change, but it had also meant the absence of the good aroma of Danish Christmas breads and cookies, pumpkin pies, and roasting goose that had made the whole house smell so wonderful in other years. The warm festive spirit of Christmas season was missing in the Carlsens' big white-frame farmhouse. The tree was a last-minute fifty-cent purchase, a lopsided little pine that could not be redeemed by its decorations. It didn't even get to have lights because none of the strings from previous years were any good, and Mamma said she couldn't waste money on Christmas lights—she hardly had enough money for electric light bulbs for the house!

Marie sighed. She might as well go upstairs and get into bed and try to sleep. At least she'd feel warmer under winter patchwork quilts.

There were four bedrooms and a bathroom upstairs. Theirs was quite a new and modern farmhouse, Marie knew, compared to the majority of farm homes in their district, which were built without electric lights or inside plumbing. The Carlsen house was built in 1918, when Lars was a baby— during the Great War Mamma had said. Papa had wanted a big family and so he had built a big house with many bedrooms. Then in 1924, when Marie was three and Karen only two months old, Papa died of a stroke. Marie could not remember Papa, so she'd never really missed him. Yet this was the house that Papa had planned, had carpenters build with oak floors and woodwork, had paid the city of Spencer to extend electricity the two miles along Highway 71 south to his farm, and had plumbers install running water. Mamma said he was so proud of the house he had built for his *barnnt* to grow up in. It was sad when Marie thought about it. Papa had lived only six years in the house he had built. Then he died and never knew how any of them grew up. Mamma said that Papa was a good farmer and a good man.

Marie thought about Papa now and wished he hadn't died. She felt certain everything would have been different if he had lived. They wouldn't be poor. Alfred and Rosie wouldn't have left home. Christmas this year wouldn't be like this.

After Rosie left home in September of 1932, the little room next to the bathroom had become Marie's room. A much larger room across the hall belonged to Lars. Karen, who was going on ten, now shared the big front bedroom with their schoolteacher sister, Cora. Alfred's bedroom, empty now, at the top of the stairs was used as a spare room for a hired man sometimes or for overnight company. Mamma's bedroom was downstairs, the one she had once shared with Papa. The closet of that bedroom had been a spooky place to hide when Marie and Karen were little, and played hide-and-seek with visiting children. In the dark recesses of that closet in a crawl space under the stairs, was real evidence that Papa had lived: straw hats and old-fashioned black shoes, boxes of things like cuff links, smoking pipes, reading glasses with gold rims, and metal-covered picture albums. This closet Mamma ruled off-limits to everyone except herself. Papa's things were to be left alone, never touched. But Marie and Karen had not been able to resist peeking into the dark depths of that forbidden location when Marie thought Mamma's back was turned.

Mamma never talked much about Papa. His picture was the only way Marie had of visualizing him in her mind. Between Rosie's and Cora's high school graduation pictures on the piano downstairs in the living room, was the picture of a man with a high forehead, deepset eyes like Alfred's, and a handlebar mustache. Sometimes when Marie dusted his picture, she looked at him very closely. Mamma said Marie looked like him. Marie knew it was the eyes. *The Carlsen eyes* Mamma called them. When she was little and was told to dust in the living room, Marie wondered if Papa could see her out of those eyes from the picture on the piano. She wondered about the spirits of people who died and went to heaven. Did they ever come back to their houses on earth? Could spirits see what people were doing? Was Papa's spirit watching her when she dusted his picture? Did he think she was growing up okay? You never knew about spirits. Marie always gave Rosie and Cora's high school graduation pictures a quick swish with the dustcloth. She was usually more painstaking with the dusting of Papa's picture. You might as well be on the safe side with spirits. Everybody in the family said she was growing up to be lazy and she really didn't want Papa, even though he was dead, to have that opinion of her, especially in regard to his picture.

Marie sat down on the cot in her bedroom and looked out the west window. She could see the barnyard of their farm from that window. The buildings were red with white trim and most of them had been built in 1927, some six years ago, after a terrible fire had burned down the old Carlsen barn. The fire had also taken the chicken house, garage, and several sheds to the ground. Mamma had carpenters rebuild the kind of barn she said Papa would have wanted. The new barn was massive with purplish fireproof brick half way up and a thick cement foundation. Marie remembered Mamma saying, "Peter always wanted buildings that could be seen from the highway. He would have been so proud of this barn with its electric lights. This is a barn that will never

8

burn to the ground. It is the kind of barn that he would want because it will remain standing on this farm for his children, grandchildren, and even for great-grandchildren. Yes, this is a building that will last for generations."

Now, in 1933, it was such a cold Christmas day that the cows and horses were inside the barn. The pigs were in the old pighouse down past the grove. There was not even a chicken or goose outside the buildings. The barnyard looked bleak and dismal, covered with cold white snow, and Marie could not imagine why Papa or Mamma, or anybody else for that matter, should get so much satisfaction out of building big barns that just meant a lot of hard work—like pitching manure and milking cows—when they never had any money to buy nice Christmas presents or even good things to eat from the grocery store. Mamma said times would get better but Marie didn't see much hope of that. Not this Christmas anyway.

Feeling cold and lonely, Marie took off her shoes and still wearing her clothes she got under the covers of Rosie's cot. *Rosie's cot!* It was her own room now. Why was it that she still thought of this room as belonging to her sister Rosie? It didn't make any difference that Rosie's things were gone. Those of her clothes and other possessions left behind had long ago been packed in boxes and stored in the attic. Marie slept in Rosie's bed, kept her things in Rosie's dresser, and hung her clothes in Rosie's closet. Time, almost a year and a half now since Rosie left home, had not dispelled the idea in Marie's mind that this was still Rosie's room. How she wished she were through high school, grown up, and could be like Rosie and live away from the farm, some place warm and nice. Rosie had lived near Hollywood for awhile! Imagine being grown up, living in California, near Hollywood!

Thoughts of present, past, and future were jumbled together in Marie's mind as she began to feel warmer and a little more comfortable under the covers. It was such a strange thing to think about. *Time.* Time built walls between what was and what might someday be; and much as Marie wished she would hurry and grow up, she found herself longing for a time that was past. Part of her wanted to go back to a time that was over and could never be again—the time before Rosie went away, before she was married to Nick and had a baby. Marie longed for the time when Rosie had lived at home, worked at the laundry in Spencer, and brought home pork and beans and sardines for Saturday supper on paydays, and laughed and joked and hugged Marie for no reason except that Rosie loved her and liked to hug. She remembered how Rosie would move over and let her get into bed with her on cold winter nights when she was afraid of the dark after getting out of Cora's bed to go to the bathroom. Rosie would draw up her knees and make a chair for her against her warm flannel nightgown-clad body and say, "You're cold as ice, Kiddo. Pretend I'm a chair and we'll be so close together we'll keep each other warm. Don't talk. Go back to sleep now. I have to get up early." Rosie's pillow always smelled like Yankee Clover cologne. It still did. Marie used the same scent so it would remind her of Rosie.

Rosie had never come back home. Maybe she never would. When Marie considered that possibility, tears began welling up in her eyes. She brushed them away impatiently. What a stupid thing to think. Of course Rosie would come home again. She'd said she would, hadn't she? And bring Nick and the baby. The trouble was that nobody knew where they were now. Letters sent before Thanksgiving to Rosie and Nick, came back marked "moved—address unknown." No letters had come from Rosie for a long, long time.

Suddenly Marie heard loud knocking on a door downstairs. The knocking became banging. Who in the world was down there?

"Marie! Marie! Are you upstairs? Are you in bed? I'm coming up so you better be decent!"

Marie recognized the voice. It was Lyle Tornquist. In a few minutes he was standing in the doorway of her bedroom carrying a napkin-covered tray.

"I told Ma I'd drive over with something for you to eat. She was afraid you'd die of starvation. I can drive the car now, Marie. If you weren't playing sick, I'd take you for a ride. You don't look so bad. I mean you've got a fat lip all right but you don't look near as goofy as Lars said you did." Lyle pulled a chair close to Marie's bed and uncovered the tray. Marie looked at Katie Tornquist's glazed ham and sweet potatoes, escalloped corn, fruit salad, and chocolate cake with fudge frosting and realized she really was about to die of starvation. There was a napkin and silverware on the tray. Lyle was smiling down at her.

Thank goodness, she'd gone back to bed with her clothes on. Marie sat up and started eating. Lyle stood by the bed, watching. "You act real sick, Marie. Real sick, eating like a horse. You want me to go downstairs and get you some water or milk or something?"

"No," said Marie, "and thanks, Lyle, if you're ever sick I'll do something nice for you. I mean it. I really will."

Lyle smiled his familiar big-dimpled smile. "Well, I'm

11

not going to hold my breath waiting for you to do something nice and I don't expect to get sick. I'll tell my ma that you look like you're going to live."

"Well, I'm not really sick, Lyle. I had a cold but it ended up in cold sores. That always happens and it makes me so mad, especially now at Christmas time."

"Yeah, I know what you mean. It's tough luck. Once I broke my arm right before Halloween and I didn't get to go out and help knock over outdoor privies or tear down any fences. That was the year Lars and Norman pushed Henry Byers's new car down in a muddy ditch. Remember? Old Henry had a terrible time pulling it out and nobody offered to help him except his pa. I guess he finally got their hired men to dig it out of the mud and use a tractor to do it. Boy, was old Henry ever mad because he never knew who did it."

Marie smiled. As far as she was concerned Henry Byers deserved any terrible thing anybody could think of to do to him. He was mean and selfish. Nobody liked him. Rosie had been engaged to Henry for a little while that summer of 1932 before she left home. Rosie didn't love Henry. But for a while she'd thought she could help out at home by marrying him. The Depression—always being poor—made people, even people like Rosie, do things they wouldn't dream of otherwise. But then Nick had come into their lives, and Rosie just couldn't settle for a life without true love. Well, even if it meant having Rosie gone, Marie was glad her sister hadn't stayed home and settled for Henry Byers.

"Red Gillette's coming to my house tomorrow. You want me to bring him over to see you, Marie?"

"Don't you dare, Lyle. This is the worst Christmas vacation I ever had."

"I thought maybe you'd want to give him a big fat kiss," Lyle teased, as laughing, he left Marie to finish eating her dinner.

It didn't even seem like Christmas this year. Being poor had spoiled the future for the whole family. Cora had decided to spend Christmas day with Milton's family. Marie wondered where Alfred and Rosie were eating their Christmas dinners. She hoped they were having a better time than she was.

Suddenly the phone rang. Two shorts and a long. Two shorts and a long. It was the Carlsen ring on the party line.

Marie decided not to answer the phone. If she'd gone along to the Tornquist house, nobody would be home now to pick up the receiver. The call would go unanswered. It was probably just somebody for Lars anyway. Lars had a lot of friends, from farms and some who lived in town, and they called and invited him to go places. Nobody ever called Marie. She probably had fewer friends than any girl her age in the world! Marie didn't feel like talking to anybody and explaining why she was the only one home on Christmas day. Whoever was on the phone could just call back later when the others were home.

The phone kept ringing, sounding more insistent each time. Finally, there seemed no choice but to get off the bed, go downstairs, walk into the dining room, and pick up the receiver.

"Hello," Marie said, aware that her voice sounded breathless from hurrying downstairs. "Hello, hello," she said, almost hoping that the person had already hung up.

"Hello! Hello!" It was Rosie's voice! Coming from far away, calling long distance! Rosie! It was really her sister calling home on Christmas day.

"Rosie!" Marie was almost yelling into the telephone. She was so afraid Rosie would hang up or the connection would be cut off. *"Rosie! Rosie! It's me. Marie."*

"Kiddo? Kiddo?" Rosie's voice seemed to come from a long way off. Long distance was like that. Sometimes it was hard to hear whoever was on the other end of the line.

"Where are you? Rosie, where are you?"

"You don't have to yell, Kiddo. I can hear you just fine. Is Mamma there? Let me talk to Mamma. I can only talk three minutes. That's all the money I have and I'm at a pay phone."

"Mamma's not here, Rosie. They all went to the Torn-quists for Christmas dinner except me. I couldn't go because I have cold sores all over my mouth. I'm home alone."

"Oh, you poor kid! I used to get them when I was your age. I remember how awful it was. Listen, Marie, tell Mamma I probably won't be able to call again. It's really hard to get through on Christmas. Just tell her Nick and I and the baby are fine. We're in Kansas City but I don't know how long we'll be here if Nick can't find a job. I got a job in a restaurant and we all get to eat here so we're not starving. We just have a sleeping room but it's clean and nice. Tell Mamma we're okay and that I wrote her a long letter and Nick mailed it for me. Did you get the letter yet?"

"No. We haven't had a letter since before Thanksgiving."

"That's funny. I gave it to Nick to mail a long time before Christmas. Maybe he forgot to mail it. I'll have to

14

ask him about it. Well, anyway, how is everybody? Do you hear from Alfred?"

"Everybody's fine, Rosie. Alfred's okay. He writes to Mamma or somebody every week. He's still in Chicago. He's just about done with his electrician school and he's trying to get a job. If he can't find one, he might come back home. Anyway that's what he said in his last letter."

"How about Cora and Milton. They planning to get married?"

"I don't know. They might as well be married. They have to be together all the time. Cora's at Milton's house today eating dinner with his family."

"Oh, I sure wish we could come home, Kiddo. Maybe we can this summer. I sure miss Mamma and all you kids and I want you to see the baby before he grows up. I'll send you some pictures. Nick got a camera and we took some of him. I think he looks a lot like Nick but he thinks Tommy looks like me. I guess he looks a little like both of us. He's got Nick's eyes and smile but I'm afraid he's got my long nose, poor kid."

"I'll bet he's cute," said Marie.

"Yes, he really is. And funny. The other day, we took him to see Santa Claus in a department store here and he. . . ."

"This is the operator . . . Your three minutes are up . . . If you wish to talk longer you must. . . ."

"Marie! I have to hang up now. Tell Mamma we're okay. I love you. Good-bye, Marie."

"Rosie! Good-bye!"

There was a click and Marie knew Rosie had hung up the receiver. I should have told her I loved her . . . that we all want her to come home and bring Nick and the baby . . . I should have asked her to give me her address or the name of the restaurant she's working at. Oh, I should have found out so Mamma could call her at the restaurant. . . . Marie felt like crying. If Rosie didn't have enough money to talk more than three minutes, why didn't she call and reverse the charges and have the call go on Mamma's telephone bill like Alfred did sometimes. But she knew Rosie was not like Alfred and she would never want Mamma to know that she didn't have enough money to call. Rosie was too proud and so good at pretending that everything was okay when it wasn't. Yet Rosie had sounded okay on the phone. She'd sounded fine.

Marie went back upstairs. She might as well go back to bed. Before she climbed into the bed, she caught a glimpse of herself in the mirror. She looked at her image with the puffed up lips. She looked hideous. Marie made a grotesque face at herself. Then she laughed. There was one good thing about having cold sores. They were the reason she'd stayed home today. Otherwise, she wouldn't have been here at home when Rosie called. How terrible if nobody had been home on Christmas day when Rosie finally got her call through. Now she could tell Mamma that they were okay and in Kansas City and they'd be getting a letter from her soon, too, Rosie had said. Maybe she'd just sleep until everybody came home from the Tornquists' house. Marie snuggled down under the covers and felt almost good.

Marie slept soundly. She did not wake up until she heard noises and voices downstairs. It was beginning to get dark outside. Getting out of bed, she picked up the tray Lyle had

16

brought with the Christmas dinner and hurried down to the kitchen. Only Mamma was in the house now. Marie knew that Lars and Karen were out in the barn doing the evening milking. Marie had never learned to milk, mainly because squeezing the milk out of a cow's udders was something she found repulsive and she'd never put forth her best effort. Karen had learned to milk when she was eight and so it was her job to help Lars in the barn.

"Cora, Rosie, and Karen all know how to milk cows. Marie isn't too dumb to learn. She's just too lazy," Lars often grumbled.

Mamma always defended Marie's dislike for barn work. Marie suspected that Mamma knew she was afraid of animals. Mamma said when she was little, older children had teased her by putting spitting barnyard cats in her arms just to hear her scream in terror, afraid to hold the cat and afraid to let it go. There was even a picture of Marie when she was three in the family album which showed her crying as she stood holding a huge tomcat around his middle. The family laughed when they looked at that picture of little Marie, scared silly of cats! Marie never laughed, even now. It still made her angry when they laughed at her childish fears.

"Guess what, Mamma?" Marie said now. "While you were gone this afternoon Rosie called long distance! She and Nick and the baby are in Kansas City. In Kansas I think or maybe Missouri. I guess she didn't say which. Anyway, Rosie's got a job working in a restaurant and Nick's looking for a job and they might come home this summer and. . . ."

"Where do they live? Did you get her phone number or her address so that I can call her?"

Marie realized now how awful it was that Mamma hadn't

17

been home when Rosie called. She couldn't tell Mamma anything she needed to know. Mamma was very upset.

"Marie, why didn't you find out how to get in touch with Rose? What is the name of the place where she works?"

"I don't know, Mamma. Rosie hung up before I got a chance to ask. She was at a pay phone and she only had enough money to talk three minutes. Mamma, she said she sent a letter and we should get it pretty soon and Nick mailed it a long time before Christmas and. . . ."

"Oh, Marie, Marie. . . ." and Mamma looked like she might cry.

It was almost the middle of January before the Christmas card and the letter from Rosie came in the mail. The letter was dated before Christmas, and the envelope was dirty and battered looking. The return address was blurred because it had been written in blue ink and it looked like the letter had gotten wet. It was a disappointing letter for all the Carlsen family because nothing was said about plans to return home.

"I'll bet old Nick never even mailed the letter when Rosie gave it to him," said Lars. "I'll bet he lost it or threw it away and somebody else found it lying in the street or someplace, put a three-cent stamp on it, and mailed it. Otherwise, why'd it take so long to get here and why's the envelope in such bad shape that we can't even read the return address?"

Nobody had the answer to those questions. Everyone in the family tried to read the address in the upper corner of the envelope, but it was no use. The only words plain enough to read were Kansas City, Kansas. There was no address to which to write on Rosie's scrawled-on-tablet-paper letter

18

folded inside the Christmas card which was simply signed, Rosie, Nick and Tommy.

Rosie's letter was brief and seemed to have been written in haste. Yet it was good to see her familiar large, rounded-letter handwriting. Rosie said that she and Nick and the baby might go to St. Louis to visit Nick's aunt after Christmas. Nick wanted her to see the baby while he was still little.

"How about us? When are we going to get to see him?" asked Marie bitterly. "It seems like all she can do is what Nick wants to do."

Mamma made no comment. She turned back to the stove and gave her attention to something she was cooking. Marie had the feeling that even though she wouldn't admit it, Mamma felt the same frustrations that she did. *When was Rosie ever coming back home?*

"Can Spring Be Far Behind?"

"LYLE, I'LL BE SO GLAD WHEN SPRING GETS HERE. I HATE winter. It's the worst time of the year, especially January and February," complained Marie as she walked along Highway 71 with Lyle toward their country schoolhouse.

"Look at it this way, Marie. 'When winter comes, can spring be far behind'?"

Lyle was laughing but Marie was not amused by the line from a poem Marie considered to be stupid. Miss Eriksen, their teacher, was great on having pupils memorize and recite poems. Marie couldn't remember who wrote the poem Lyle was quoting from but she knew it wasn't likely to be anything written by Longfellow. Henry Wadsworth Longfellow wrote *good* poems. Marie loved "Hiawatha" and "The Children's Hour."

"Farmers in Iowa need cold weather and a lot of snow

in order to have good corn crops," said Lyle seriously now. You know that, Marie, so stop complaining about a few months of winter. Spring and summer are always nice and it really isn't going to be long now before spring will be here."

That was the good thing about Lyle. Even on a day like today when the wind was sharp against their faces and the freezing cold snow was piled high in ditches, Lyle could find something to be cheerful about. Lyle was in eighth grade and Marie was in seventh. They were friends. Better friends this year than ever before because Lars and Lyle's brother Norman were now going to high school in Spencer and so it was Marie and Lyle who walked to and from school together. Karen was in fourth grade and usually ran ahead of them. She had no interest in Marie and Lyle's conversations.

"Do you think you'll live in Iowa when you're through school, Lyle?" asked Marie. "I mean do you think you'd want to be a farmer like your father?"

"Nope," said Lyle, "I'm going to be an airplane pilot. As soon as I graduate from high school, I'm going to join the air corps. I want to fly like my Uncle Rollie."

Marie knew that Rollie Tornquist, Lyle's uncle who lived in St. Louis, had been a pilot in the World War and now owned his own private plane. Last summer he had flown it to the Spencer airport which had recently been built along Highway 71, close to the Tornquist and Carlsen farms. Lars and Marie had gone to the airport with Lyle to see his Uncle Rollie's airplane. It was red and yellow and had an open cockpit. Rollie had a brown leather jacket and helmet. Marie thought he even looked a little like Charles Lindbergh with his curly hair but when he smiled, he showed big dimples

21

like Lyle's. Lyle had begged him to take him up in the plane and his Uncle Rollie had laughed. "Sorry, Lyle, I can't. I promised your ma I wouldn't. Katie would kill me if I took any kids up in this plane. You know how she is about flying."

That was the only time Marie had known Lyle to really get mad at his mother. "Well, someday I'm going to fly and there won't be one thing she can do to stop me," Lyle had grumbled but Marie had understood Katie's fears. She could think of nothing more frightening than to get into that rickety little plane and go up into the sky. What if the engine stopped? What if it had a leaking gas tank? What if the landing gear came loose or broke off? Who could fix anything that went wrong? Nobody! The plane would crash and everybody in it would get killed. Yet Lyle had none of these fears. His biggest interest in life was airplanes. He drew them, read about them, and every chance he got he went to the Spencer airport and looked at them and sometimes the airport manager would let him sit in the cockpit of a plane that was in the hangar or on the ground. In the summertime, when Marie was bored and had nothing better to do, she'd gone to the airport with Lyle and watched planes take off or land while Lyle asked questions of the pilots or the airport manager about flying.

Red Gillette, Lyle's friend from a farm in another school district in Riverton Township, often came to the Tornquist farm to visit Lyle. Red was not interested in airplanes. He intended to be a farmer like his father, Matt.

Red had told Lyle that he liked Marie and once he had even told her so himself. Red was in eighth grade and Marie could not get over feeling shy and nervous if she ever had to talk to Red alone. She needed Lyle around in order to

22

feel comfortable. Marie hated this about herself. Would she always be like this? Afraid to talk to boys she liked and who said they liked her? How could she ever have a boyfriend, *a real boyfriend,* not just a neighbor friend like Lyle, if she never got over being so bashful and self-conscious? Marie realized that this problem was so personal, so silly, and so childish that she couldn't talk to anybody about it, not even Miss Eriksen or Mamma.

She probably could have told Rosie how she felt around Red Gillette and Rosie would have understood and maybe been able to tell her what to do about it. Rosie wouldn't make a big deal about it like Cora probably would. Cora would get her a book about developing self-confidence or something. Marie was sure books wouldn't help. How Marie missed Rosie and their talks!

Now, as she and Lyle approached the schoolyard by the mailbox corner, Marie wished she were in eighth grade instead of seventh. If she were in eighth like Lyle, this would be her last year of country school. She would graduate at the township picnic in May. Never again would she have to walk along Highway 71 to a rural school. She would be able to do all the exciting things that high school students did. She would be considered grown up. She would be popular. She would go to football and basketball games, have movie dates, act in plays, and she'd have all kinds of girlfriends who lived in town. Life would be so much better after she started high school. The girls who went to the country school were okay but they were boring. To tell the truth, Lyle Tornquist was more interesting to talk with than any of the girls her age in school. None of them longed to go to high school. All they ever expected to do was be a farmer's wife and nobody needed to go to high school to be that!

There was one thing that happened every Saturday that January and February of 1934 that considerably brightened up Marie's life. That was confirmation class at the Danish Lutheran Church on Saturday morning between ten and twelve o'clock. She had to go! Mamma insisted that every child of hers, when it was time for their Sunday school class to do it, take religious instruction from Reverend Norgaard and learn catechism, Bible history, and the doctrines of the Danish Lutheran Church of America. There were three boys and five girls, including Marie, in Marie's confirmation class, which would have instruction every Saturday for almost a year and a half until May of 1935. Then they would be confirmed as adult members of the church with all the church member privileges including contributing to the financial support of the church with their own personal church envelopes. Reverend Norgaard spent quite a lot of time explaining the obligation of financial support and how much it cost in cold hard cash to heat a church in winter. That's why on Saturday mornings in winter they had to sit around him in a circle by the church kitchen cookstove in the basement. Marie noticed that Reverend Norgaard himself managed always to sit in the chair closest to the warm stove.

Marie wore her coat all during the class on cold winter Saturday mornings and wished she didn't have to take off her mittens in order to turn the pages of the Bible. She was always glad when Reverend Norgaard said after looking at the gold pocket watch hanging from a chain, "I see it is now twelve o'clock. You may go."

That was the redeeming thing about having to go to confirmation class on Saturday morning. You could go to town every single Saturday. In fact, you *had* to go to town! Marie could suffer through confirmation class as long as it meant getting away from the farm and going into Spencer and enjoying herself after the two hours of reciting lessons and listening to the preacher was over.

Reverend Norgaard could be mean as anything and bawled anybody out who didn't know the lesson. Marie never took a chance. She'd never forgotten her humiliation when the preacher one Sunday when she was ten, in front of the whole Sunday school, had called upon her to explain the meaning of the word *covet*. She said she didn't know. Reverend Norgaard had taught her the lesson never to be unprepared for his questions by making her go down and sit on a little red chair with the three year olds in the baby class for the rest of the Sunday school period. Marie had hated the preacher ever since. It even diminished her interest in Bible study if the preacher, who was supposed to know it all, could be such a creep about what he knew and a kid didn't. She knew the "Lord's Prayer" and it said to forgive trespasses but the preacher had trespassed against her sense of justice and Marie had never forgiven him. So Marie found no pleasure in taking catechism instruction from Reverend Norgaard. Yet she never failed to answer his questions with the exact words from the book. She memorized her answers and he was satisfied.

If all the kids in the Danish Lutheran Sunday School knew better than to come to Reverend Norgaard unprepared, one girl in the Saturday confirmation class did not! That was Ethel Jorth. She was a new girl who'd moved to Spencer from Omaha, Nebraska. She was very pretty with short curly blond hair. She had the nerve to giggle when she got bawled out! Reverend Norgaard could not intimidate Ethel and his red face would get even redder and his ice blue eyes would look even colder. And Ethel would continue to giggle. Marie liked her. They became friends and after class they would go to the Rexall Drug Store and read magazines about movie stars until Lars came to drive Marie home.

"Hi, Marie." There was no mistake. Taller now but still with freckles, red hair, and his mean little grin, it was Red Gillette. "You going to run in the seventh and eighth grade races at the township picnic this year?"

"I don't know," said Marie. "I haven't decided."

"Well, if you do, you won't win!"

"Who says?"

"I do," said Red Gillette and walked away.

"Who was that, Marie?" asked Ethel Jorth. "He's kind of cute and I think he likes you."

"It's Red Gillette. He's a jerk and I hate him. He's in eighth grade and we don't go to the same school. I beat him once in a foot race and it just about killed him. I'm not going to run against him this year. Who cares about winning a stupid foot race?"

"Marie Carlsen, you're blushing," Ethel giggled. "You like him! You can't fool me. You like him and you're blushing but that's okay. He's pretty darn cute!"

When she was riding back to the farm with Lars, Marie tried to sort out her feelings about Red Gillette. Why did she keep thinking about how he'd come up to her by the magazine racks and said "Hi, Marie," while she was with Ethel when he hadn't paid any attention to her for such a long time? But Ethel was right. He was growing up to be kind of cute! Soon now it would be spring and time for the township picnic!

During the winter months, Lars was able to go to high school and still manage to do evening and morning chores. With the help of neighborhood friends—Norman and Lyle Tornquist and Homer Merkel—other farmwork could be done on weekends. With spring just around the corner, it was now necessary to find a hired man to plow, cultivate, and plant the fields with oats, corn, and alfalfa. Fences needed mending. Barns and sheds needed cleaning and painting. The driveway needed gravel and grass needed cutting. Mamma needed a farmhand.

In March, Uncle Chris drove into the Carlsen farmyard accompanied by Hans Petersen, a man he had met at the Danish Brotherhood Lodge meeting place. He had come recently from Denmark and needed a place to live, and since he spoke only Danish and preferred to live with a family who would understand his language, he was willing to work for room and board and a little spending money. Mamma was quick to accept his offer.

Hans Petersen moved into Alfred's room at the top of the stairs. He was not at all like Magnus Hansen, who had been big and exuberant, and who had lived with the Carlsens after Alfred went to Chicago. Magnus had been eager to learn English and American customs, so eager in fact that after corn picking was over in 1933, he'd left for Des Moines to go to Grandview College, which had been established before the turn of the century for the education of Danish immigrants. Hans talked to Mamma in Danish and also to Lars who understood him. He was a hard worker and knew a lot about farming but not much about being sociable. Marie decided that was probably because he was old, at least forty, and not interested in movies or radio because he couldn't understand English and didn't care to learn.

Sometimes Magnus wrote a letter to the Carlsen family in English. "Des Moines is not Copenhagen, by a long shot, but it has Spencer beat by a big country mile," Magnus wrote and Marie missed Magnus who had a way of making everyone laugh with his observations, which he liked to express in American slang. Marie was as glad when she found a letter or postcard in the mail from Magnus in Des Moines as she was from Alfred in Chicago. Alfred said he would finish his electrician course in May and if he couldn't find a job, he planned to head out West. He had a friend with a car who wanted to go to California if he could get a couple of guys to help him drive. Alfred was seriously considering going with him, visit Uncle Jens in Long Beach, and see what prospects were for work in California.

"Anything in the mail from Rose?" Mamma would ask when Marie brought the mail when she came from school at noon.

"No," Marie would say. "Not today."

Marie knew how disappointed Mamma always was as she sighed and turned back to the stove. It made Marie a little mad at Rosie. Alfred takes time to write. Even Magnus writes! Why can't Rosie write to Mamma? Marie kept these thoughts to herself because Mamma was probably thinking the same thing.

28

♫ 3 ♫

The Kid from Town

"MARIE, COME QUICK! THERE'S A FAT GIRL WITH RED HAIR downstairs buying a chicken with her mother!"

Karen was breathless from having run upstairs. Marie was lying on the bed and she'd been reading a good book, *David Copperfield*. Now she put the book down on the bed beside her and looked at her sister with annoyance.

"Who cares if there's a kid from town downstairs? They just come out to buy something and they never stay long. Why do you always bother me about such stupid things? You made me lose my place," and Marie reached for her book.

"But Marie, I want you to see her. This girl is a lot different. She doesn't act stuck-up and neither does her mother. I don't think they're rich at all. This girl is older than you I think. At least she looks older, maybe even fifteen or sixteen, and she acts nice. She smiled and said hello to me!"

Marie smiled. Karen was almost ten now, growing tall but still the eager towheaded child who got excited over the smallest thing or event. Karen also cared not a fig how she looked today or any day. She was wearing one of her old everyday dresses made out of cotton print feed sacks. She was barefoot and her feet were dirty but this did not seem to worry Karen in the least.

"Please, Marie, come on. Hurry before she leaves. Let's go down and talk to her. Maybe we can show her Mouser's kittens."

So that was it. Marie understood now. Karen needed her, a twelve-year-old sister, to make the overture of friendship. Karen was too bashful.

"All right," Marie said. "I guess I'll go down and see what she looks like. Did she ever come here before?"

"I don't think so. I never saw her before." Karen pulled Marie's hand, urging her to hurry downstairs before the girl left the house.

Downstairs the plump red-haired girl was standing by the kitchen table beside her mother who was drinking coffee with Mrs. Carlsen. The girl did seem to be in her teens and she looked like her mother. They both had curly hair of an almost orange shade, green-blue eyes, and very fair skin. They were fat, but not *too fat,* and they were dressed in cotton print dresses. If they weren't rich, they did not appear to be especially poor either. Marie smiled and said hello to the strangers and both mother and daughter responded warmly to her greeting. At least they were friendly which was more than could be said for most people who came to the Carlsen farm to buy produce. Usually, the kids from town sat in their mother's shiny new cars and would stare curiously at Marie if she were in the barnyard. Only the mother would get out of the car and she would follow Mamma around and look at the chickens. Then she'd pick out a spring chicken or roasting hen. After the people left, Mamma would catch it, chop off its head, put it in boiling water, and pluck and dress it. Rich ladies from town were not like Mamma. They could never dress a chicken! Marie wondered if the red-haired woman had asked Mamma to do it and would return for it later as other customers did.

"I didn't realize you had any children this young," said the woman looking at Marie and Karen.

"Oh, yes, Marie was three years old and Karen only two months when Peter died. That was almost ten years ago and they are starting to grow up now too. Time flies by so fast," said Mamma. "How old is your girl now, Erma? She was such a little one when you moved away."

"Gertrude Caroline is fifteen," said the woman, "and as you can see, she's not a little girl anymore."

"You can say that again, Ma," laughed the girl.

Mamma laughed too. "Yes, they can't stay babies for long. Marie is almost thirteen and Karen is almost ten. It just doesn't seem possible. Marie will go into high school in town after one more year of grade school. Time goes so fast."

"Gertrude Caroline graduated from eighth grade when she was thirteen but she didn't go on to high school. I felt so bad about that, but it was just too hard for my husband to drive her from the farm into the town high school. Some say it's not so important for a girl to go on in school but I always say education never hurts anybody and the more you get the better you're off in the long run."

Then after Marie and Karen stared at Gertrude Caroline

and her mother for awhile and after the mother told about how smart the girl was without going to high school, Karen went over to Mamma and whispered something in her ear.

Mamma smiled. "They want to take Gertrude Caroline out to the barn and show her the kittens," Mamma laughed.

Marie was mortified. *They* Mamma had said. She made it sound like she was just as big a baby as Karen, too bashful to ask for herself. And even worse, as if she, like Karen, thought the biggest thing in life was to show somebody a bunch of cats. Marie wished she had never come downstairs to get a look at the kid from town.

"Ma, you said we couldn't stay long," said the girl in a gruff voice—almost like a boy's. "I don't think we have time for me to look at the cats."

"Well, I do have to settle up with Mrs. Carlsen for the chickens," said the woman. "How much do I owe you?"

Marie watched her take a little coin purse out of her worn pocketbook and start counting out some change.

"Put your money away," said Mamma. "You can pay me after your husband finds work."

"I don't like to owe money," said the woman but she snapped the coin purse shut. "You can be sure I'll pay as soon as we're a little better off."

"Times are hard, Erma," said Mamma. "It is too bad you lost your farm but you were lucky to have a home to come back to. It may take a while but your husband will get a job if he keeps looking. They don't pay much but there are still some jobs to be found if a man is willing to work for next to nothing."

"Well, we'd better be going," said the woman.

"Finish your coffee, Erma," said Mamma. "It's so nice to see you again after all these years. Your mother and I were good friends and we miss her at church. Time goes by so fast."

They started talking about times before the woman's mother and father had died. They drank their coffee and talked about people that Marie had never known.

"Come on," said Gertrude Caroline in her gruff voice. "Let's go out and look at the cats."

"Yes, you run along with the girls," said her mother, "but don't be gone long and don't step in manure in your good shoes."

"Oh, boy," said the girl as they walked out the back door, "she acts like I don't have the brains I was born with— 'don't step in manure in your good shoes,' " she mimicked. Then she laughed her throaty laugh. "You be careful," she said to Karen. "It's a hell of a lot worse to step in manure without shoes than with them. Come on, show me the crazy cats."

They walked toward the barn, past a battered old Ford with a crate containing two sqawking chickens on the back seat. It was plain to Marie now that the woman did not intend for Mamma to kill, pluck, or dress the chickens. Of course if she'd lived on a farm she could do it herself. Farm women had to do things like that and it was just one reason that Marie wanted to go to high school. So she wouldn't have to marry a farmer when she grew up. Maybe it was okay for some girls but Marie had decided long ago that life on the farm was not the kind of future she'd want. That's why she'd always looked forward to going to high school and learning enough to leave home and work in town, clerk in a store if nothing else.

"Boy, your ma is sure nice," said Gertrude Caroline now, motioning toward the squawking chickens in the car. "Ma didn't know if we could afford even one chicken and she caught us two for the same price. We haven't had fried chicken for a long time."

"We got lots of chickens," said Karen.

"We've got some too on the acreage," said Gertrude Caroline, "but they're layers. If we butcher our layers, we wouldn't have any eggs. Sure nice of your ma to catch us a couple of springs."

"We just eat springs too," said Marie. "I don't think anybody butchers layers."

"Not unless they're nuts," said Gertrude Caroline, "and let me tell you, there are plenty of those in this world. Old Jake wants us to eat rabbits. Boy, is he nuts!"

"Who's Jake?" asked Marie, because she liked to know whom somebody was talking about.

"My lame-brained stepfather."

"Is your real father dead?" asked Karen, "because ours is and we don't have a stepfather either."

"You're probably better off without one," said Gertrude Caroline. "I don't know if my old man is alive or dead and I don't care. He took off when I was a baby and he never came back. First my mother kept house for old Jake and then she married him. Now she's stuck with him. You kids are lucky you don't have a stepfather like old Jake. He's nuts!"

Marie had just finished reading about how cruel and mean David Copperfield's stepfather was to him. She had been thankful that Mamma had never married again after Papa died. What if Mamma had married somebody like David's stepfather, Mr. Murdstone. How terrible that would be! Now Gertrude Caroline was telling them that she had a stepfather who was nuts! Life could be even worse Marie decided. Maybe she was lucky after all.

"We have to climb the ladder to the haymow," said Karen. "That's where the baby kittens are, in the haymow."

"Okay. You two go up first. Just lead the way," said Gertrude Caroline. "I'm getting a little big to climb ladders and it'll take me a little longer. To tell the truth I've seen enough cats to last a lifetime. I was getting sick of listening to Ma talk about her life history. Whenever she calls me Gertrude Caroline in that dripping honey voice, I feel like screaming. I guess she thinks it makes me sound ladylike which is one thing I'm not. I'm Trudy! Not Gertrude Caroline! Except of course when Ma feels like putting on the dog. I just want you to know my name is Trudy Horton so don't ever call me Gertrude, or Gertie, or Gert! Every time my ma puts on her phony-baloney act I have to set things straight. Otherwise I get called names I can't stand and I mean *Gertrude Caroline!*"

"Okay, Trudy," said Marie and considered that the name was one that suited the red-haired kid much better than the one she'd been given at birth. Marie had never known a girl as outspoken and tough-acting as Trudy Horton but maybe she grew up that way having somebody like old Jake for a stepfather.

Trudy was puffing a little from climbing the haymow ladder and mounting the piles of straw to the corner where the mother cat had hidden her kittens.

"See, aren't they cute, Trudy?" said Karen. "You can't touch them though. I just found them yesterday and they don't have their eyes open yet."

Six little kittens of various descriptions (black and white, gray and white, some with spots and some with stripes, and one all white) were nestled in the straw by the black and white mother cat.

"Cute as can be," said Trudy. "Do you suppose I could have one. I'd sure be tickled to have the little white one if you plan to give them away."

Marie knew that pure white barnyard kittens were rare and that Karen would be reluctant to give it away. She waited to see how her sister would answer Trudy's request. Karen had always been a generous little girl but not when it came to parting with a favorite cat.

"It's too little to give away. It has to stay with its mother until it gets bigger."

"That's okay. I know that. When it gets old enough to leave the mother cat, I'll come back out and get it. You wouldn't want to leave it running loose in the barn anyway. It could get stepped on by a cow or a horse. We don't have any cats now and I'd take very good care of it. Really I would," promised Trudy.

"All right," said Karen, "but it will be a lot of weeks before it will be time to leave its mother."

When they left the barn, Erma Horton and Mrs. Carlsen were standing beside the car with the sqawking chickens.

"Hurry up and get in the car," said Trudy's mother. "You'll have to help butcher the chickens when we get home."

Trudy waved to them as her mother drove out of the

driveway. When the three of them walked back to the house, Mamma did not seem to notice that Karen was unusually quiet and that she was blinking back tears. Marie noticed but she just went back upstairs to continue reading *David Copperfield*. Karen did not follow her and Marie felt sure Karen was sorry she'd shown the kittens to the kid from town.

4

Growing Up Doesn't Mean Forgetting

THAT SPRING OF 1934 IT SEEMED TO MARIE THAT THEY HAD a hundred cats. Every one of them belonged to Karen and had names like Blackie, Whitey, or Spotty—names Karen had given them, not always imaginative—but every single cat was named. There were Goldie, Brownie, Tiger, Mouser, Bobby, Johnny, Wildcat, Dagwood, Wimpy, Jiggs. There was a never-ending list of comic strip characters with namesakes among Karen's cat population. Karen kept close track of cat pregnancies.

Skeezix was a reddish, part-Persian cat which Rosie had found as a kitten, hungry and lost, in an alley behind the laundry where she'd worked. It was a cute little kitten and Rosie had brought it home for Karen. Nobody had taken the trouble to investigate its sex and Karen had given it the name Skeezix after a red-haired funny paper character. Later she learned that Skeezix was not a "boy cat" but was going to be a mother. But this didn't sway Karen.

"Skeezix is skinny again! *He's had his kittens!* Come on, Marie, let's go hunt for them!"

Marie was urged to stop reading. She'd finished *Little Women,* one of the books Cora had brought home from the town library. Cora checked out armloads of books for the country school kids she taught in Summit Township. Now Marie was reading *Little Men* but, unlike *Little Women,* it did not always hold her interest. For that reason, today she felt more tolerant of Karen's interruption. Besides, Skeezix was rather a special cat having been found by Rosie. Marie, no longer afraid, had even taken her turn feeding Skeezix with milk from an eye dropper until he'd been old enough to lap up the cow's milk with the rest of Karen's barnyard cats.

Secretly, Marie had to admit that even she enjoyed the adventure of searching for baby kittens. Mother cats came up with such ingenious hiding places. Then there were the questions that would be answered at the end of the search. How many would there be? What would they look like? Would they have their eyes open?

Skeezix had hidden her kittens well. For days Marie and Karen followed the cat around hoping to be led to the kittens. Marie began to fear that a tomcat or a rat had found them first. Lars had told them that they sometimes ate newborn kittens. Marie did not tell Karen her fears. They kept on looking.

After several days, Marie gave up hope of finding Skeezix's kittens. Karen continued to search. Marie felt either they'd been hidden especially well by a very clever mother cat . . . or the worst of her fears had happened. No need to tell Karen.

But one morning when Marie came down for breakfast, Karen was crying.

"No," said Cora who was helping Mamma cook breakfast, "you know she wouldn't do a thing like that. Lars doesn't know what he's talking about."

"She did too! I know she drowned Skeezix's kittens! I saw it from the bathroom window. She was down by the tank with a gunnysack. I saw you down there, Mamma! Lars said you put a rock in the sack with the kittens and put them in the tank."

A look passed between Cora and Mamma. And Marie knew what Karen said was true.

Mamma tried to hold Karen. But she wouldn't let her.

"I hate you," said Karen and ran outside.

"Where's Lars?" said Cora. "I'd like to get my hands on him. She wouldn't have known what you were doing if he hadn't told her. What makes him so mean?"

"Don't blame Lars," sighed Mamma. "He didn't know she'd take it this way. He's still young and he expected her to understand. He was up doing chores and he must have seen from the barn. She went out looking for them as soon as she came down this morning and I suppose he told her there was no use. I didn't tell him he shouldn't tell her because I didn't think anyone saw. No, don't blame your brother, Cora. He didn't know."

"She'll cry for awhile. But she'll get over it," said Cora.

"Yes," said Mamma, "she has to grow up. Even the babies must grow up—but it's so hard. She's only nine and it's so

40

hard for a little girl to understand. I had to do it, Cora! We have to sell our milk and we get so little money for it that we cannot afford to give so much to the cats. A whole pail a day isn't even enough for them. There are just too many! You know how they crowd around the back steps of the house mewing for scraps. They are all so thin and act half-starved. No, it would be worse to let the kittens live; but little Karen cannot be expected to understand that."

"Yes, I know," said Cora. "It's just too bad you had to drown them. Especially since they were Skeezix's kittens. Karen was so excited about looking for them and she told me she was going to write and tell Rosie all about them when she found them."

"Oh, Cora," sighed Mamma. "I wish now I'd let them live. I should have understood that those kittens were special because Rose gave her that cat. I found them down in the threshing machine shed this morning when I was looking for eggs. It was so early, I thought she was still asleep. I never once thought about her being up and looking out of the bathroom window."

Suddenly Marie remembered that she had seen something bad happening, too, once when she was looking out of the bathroom window. It had been several years ago when she was about Karen's age. It had been in the wintertime and now as she remembered, Marie had the same sick feeling in her stomach as she had that morning so long ago. The whole scene was vivid in her memory.

The bathroom window upstairs provided a view of the farmyard. It was just a natural reaction to look out the window if it was light enough to see anything. She'd had to get up very early that morning to use the toilet. The sun hadn't come up but the moon was so bright you could see everything in a strange and spooky way. The trees had looked like black skeletons standing so still in the cold white snow.

Then Marie noticed swift movement across the snow. It was a huge, dark, wolflike wild dog running toward the driveway with something in its mouth—a chicken. And it was still alive, moving in the dog's mouth. Trying to get away, but caught between the dog's teeth! Marie knew the horrible kind of dog that had come into their yard that night was a chicken killer dog. Sometimes they ran in packs, like wolves, wild and homeless. They entered chicken houses at night when people were sleeping. If a farmer ever saw a chicken killer dog, he would shoot it if he could get his gun fast enough. The dog with the chicken in his mouth was quickly out of sight but the cruel scene remained in Marie's memory.

She'd gone back to bed, and for a long time she couldn't get back to sleep thinking about the evil of things that happened before daylight. In the morning, Mamma sent her out to the pump to get a pail of water and she'd seen spots of blood in the snow. Marie had felt sick to her stomach again and she couldn't eat any breakfast.

It was so long ago—almost three years ago—that she'd seen the dog killing the chicken. She should have forgotten by now, but as she sat at the kitchen table and listened to Mamma talk to Cora about Karen being too small to understand, Marie knew she would never forget!

All Mamma and Cora knew how to do was stand around and talk about Karen which wouldn't do any good at all. Marie got up from the table and went out to look for Karen.

She wasn't hard to find. Marie knew the places to look for her. Karen was sitting in the oats bin and she was holding the skinny Skeezix on her lap.

"Why?" she asked Marie. "Why did she drown Skeezix's kittens? I wanted Skeezix's kittens most of all." Karen's face was dirt-streaked with tears.

"She had a reason. Mamma had a reason. She said we have too many cats and there's not enough milk for them."

"No, we've got a lot of milk! She just wanted them to be dead. I hate her. I hate Mamma! I'm going to run away. I'm going to take Skeezix and run away. She's never going to drown any more of his kittens."

Karen wouldn't come out of the oats bin. Marie sat down beside her and talked to her for a long time that day. Finally Marie made Karen promise not to run away and, carrying Skeezix, she went back to the house with Marie.

That evening when Marie went upstairs to go to the toilet, she looked out the bathroom window. She could see the sun going down behind the pighouse roof. She could see the big watering tank where Mamma had drowned Skeezix's kittens. Mamma wasn't a mean person, and she was right about there being too many cats and not enough milk to feed so many. But Mamma was wrong about one thing and so was Cora. Karen would never get over feeling bad about the drowning of the kittens. She would remember looking out the bathroom window and seeing something awful, just as Marie would always remember the dog with the bleeding chicken in its mouth.

Marie remembered more as she looked out the bathroom window at the pighouse roof. She remembered that hot August day almost two years ago, in 1932 when she was still eleven. She remembered how hard she had cried the day Mrs. Merkel and her newborn baby had died. She'd cried on the pighouse roof until Rosie came down to get her and talked to her about death and said how it couldn't be helped. She'd understood. Rosie was right. Death was a bad thing no matter whether it happened to a chicken, a kitten, or a person. But you had to try to understand if you could. Anyway, she hoped she'd helped Karen by talking to her the way Rosie had that day on the pighouse roof. You need somebody older who understands how you feel to talk to when something really terrible happens. Mamma didn't know and Cora wouldn't understand either that to Karen, kittens were just as important as babies. They didn't understand because they couldn't remember what it was like to find out terrible things happened for no reason. For no reason at all that you could believe.

❧ 5 ❧

"Don't Overlook Me!"

ONE SATURDAY, AFTER CONFIRMATION CLASS, MARIE LIStened to Cora and Mamma talk about the Hortons. Cora was almost twenty-five now and she could remember—when she was a kid about Marie's age she said—when Erma Horton left town with her baby. Marie was in the dining room and Mamma and Cora were in the kitchen. She was sure they didn't know she was listening to them talk or they wouldn't have said all they did.

"Erma was so wild. Nobody was surprised when she got pregnant. He worked on a road construction gang according to the gossip," Mamma said. "Poor Gertrude. She was such a good person and she wanted to keep Erma and the baby at home with them. It was Erma's father who couldn't take the disgrace and all the talk when the man didn't show up for the wedding. I was at the church and it was so sad. I remember how. . . ."

Then the phone rang and Marie answered it. It was Erma Horton and she wanted to talk to Mamma. When she hung up the receiver, Mamma was smiling. "Erma asked if Gertrude Caroline could lead their cow out here. I said she should tell the girl to walk the cow in the ditch because of cars. Erma said she'd tell her that but she was sure Gertrude Caroline could manage a cow. After all she grew up on a farm even if it wasn't along a highway. You run along and help Trudy with the cow, Marie."

"Can I go too, Mamma?" cried Karen who had by now overcome her hostility toward Mamma for drowning the kittens. Lars, feeling some guilt about the whole episode, had told Karen that Skeezix was too young to feed a brood of kittens and most likely would have gotten weak and sick from the effort and would probably have died—and the kittens as well—from starvation. "Ma probably saved Skeezix's life by drowning her kittens," Lars had theorized and Karen had believed him.

Now Marie and Karen trudged along Highway 71 through the grass and weeds in the ditch to meet Trudy and the cow. When they got to the junction with the old gravel road, they saw the plump, red-haired figure struggling to pull the cow's head up from the grass along the shoulder. As they neared the place where the cow and girl stood, Marie could hear Trudy shouting.

"Come on, Beauty, gosh darn you. We haven't got all day!"

Each time Trudy tugged on the rope and swore at the cow, she managed to get it to take a few steps. Then the cow would stop again, stretch its head toward the ditch, and eat more grass.

"Damn your dirty red hide, Beauty," yelled Trudy. "You want to bloat, you stupid cow?"

"How come you're bringing your cow to our farm, Trudy?" asked Karen.

"To be with your bull."

"But why?" Karen persisted.

"So she'll have a calf and come fresh with milk."

Karen still didn't understand. "But how could just being with our bull make her do that?"

"For a farm kid, you sure are dumb," said Trudy and Marie was shocked to hear Trudy explain to Karen exactly what kind of relationship Beauty would have with the Carlsen bull.

It was one thing for Trudy to talk about such things with somebody like herself who was almost thirteen and knew about matters of sex. It was something entirely different to talk about anything so crude and vulgar with Karen who was only nine. Marie began to wonder if Trudy Horton was maybe a lot tougher than she had seemed the day she'd come with her mother to buy the chickens.

"Your cow sure is strong!" Marie said to change the subject. It took all three of them to keep Beauty moving through the grassy ditch along Highway 71. A passing motorist honked his horn at them. Trudy put her hands on her hips and yelled loud enough for him to hear, "Look me over, brother! But don't overlook me!"

So, Trudy was loud, crude, and forward! Shocked, Marie really didn't know what to think of her. She was different from any girl she'd ever known. One thing was for sure! Trudy was tough!

"You know any cute farm guys living around here?" she asked Marie as they took the cow into the barn.

"No," said Marie. "Not that well."

"Marie, you do so know cute farm boys," Karen cried. "How about Lyle Tornquist? George Knight? Homer Merkel? And what about Red Gillette? *Marie just loves Red Gillette!* Of course he doesn't live near here. He lives on a farm west of town so Marie only gets to see him when he comes to visit Lyle. Or else sometimes she sees him at 4-H meetings uptown under the bank or if there's a township picnic or something or. . . ."

"Karen, I think I hear Ma calling you," Marie lied, "I bet some kid is calling on the phone for you . . . better hurry up and go see."

"I didn't hear anybody calling," said Trudy as Karen ran toward the house.

"Ma doesn't yell very loud," said Marie.

"My ma sure can! Yell, I mean, especially when she's mad. I'll bet people can hear her a mile away."

Marie tied the cow to a stall, and she and Trudy walked out of the barn. It was early afternoon and Marie saw Lyle and Lars coming from the field, driving a team of horses hitched to a manure spreader. Marie had to admit to herself that they were both growing up to be good looking. Lars was dark-haired and tanned, muscles bulging beneath his rolled up blue denim shirt sleeves; even in overalls Lars looked okay. Lyle was the one who was really cute with his curly blond hair, brown eyes, and big dimples whenever he smiled, which was often. Of course Marie had always known Lyle so he was almost a brother to her. Marie had no romantic interest in Lyle.

As the boys drove the team closer to the barn, Trudy

whistled—like a boy!—a long drawn out sign of appreciation. "Talk about cute farm boys!" she exclaimed. *"Who are they?"*

"Just my brother Lars and his best friend, Lyle Tornquist. Lyle lives across the road."

"Well, I'm just going to have to get acquainted with your brother and your neighbor. They're both plenty cute!"

"You want to meet them now?"

"God no," said Trudy. "I look like hell. Haven't got any make-up on, feel hot and sweaty, and my hair is a mess. I'll wait until a more opportune moment as the saying goes."

Marie really didn't think that Lars would be interested in Trudy no matter how she fixed herself up. Lars didn't like fat girls and since he'd started going to high school a lot of town girls liked him. As for Lyle—Lyle wasn't interested in girls. Period. Lyle didn't seem to care if a girl was his age, older, or as young as Karen. He just didn't care about girls in a romantic way.

Marie didn't tell Trudy any of this. "Let her find out for herself," she thought as Trudy walked down the long evergreen-lined driveway, out of the Carlsen yard, toward town and her new home on the acreage.

After Trudy left, Marie went upstairs to her bedroom. She didn't feel much like reading but there was nothing else to do on Saturday afternoon except work. She never did that unless she had to. When she'd come home from town with Lars after confirmation class was over, Cora had already cleaned both upstairs and downstairs because she wanted to spend the afternoon hanging around with her boyfriend, Milton Hayes, while he clerked in the hardware store. Mamma would never let Marie stay in town with Ethel Jorth and Cora never wanted her to go to town with her. Marie was stuck at home with nothing to do!

Marie was sure nobody in the family was as bored staying home on the farm as she was. Mamma was usually busy, sewing or working in the garden, but sometimes she rested on the davenport while she read the Danish-language magazines that came in the mail. Lars and Lyle enjoyed working together so much that they didn't mind doing farm work. When Lars finished the farm work, he was sure to go over to the Tornquists and help Lyle and Norman and then they would all go into town or some place together. They went places boys liked to go to and they never invited Marie to go with them and she never asked. Karen had her cats and the other farm animals that she loved to play with and take care of on weekends.

Marie felt lonely. She was so lonely for somebody to talk with, really talk, she felt like crying. If only she knew somebody who was full of fun like her sister Rosie. Somebody who liked to laugh and share secrets. Somebody who was always around to do things with on Saturday and Sunday. Maybe Trudy, but no, Trudy was a kid from town. Besides there was something about Trudy that Marie didn't like very much. Trudy acted too tough! She swore. Nice girls never talked like Trudy. Once Rosie had told her that life was hard and you had to be tough in order to take all the hard knocks life handed out. That was the time she'd told her about how hard it was for her when Papa died when Rosie was a kid. Rosie had once told Marie that she was tough, tough as they come! But that wasn't true. Rosie never talked or acted as tough as Trudy Horton. Rosie was never loud or vulgar. She just liked to laugh and have fun. Rosie was exactly the way Marie hoped she would be when she grew up and went to high school and started having dates and going to parties and dances.

It was the middle of April now and there had been no letter from Rosie since the one with the Christmas card in the envelope that looked like it had been wet. Hard as she had tried, Marie could never make out the blurred handwriting in blue ink in the corner of the envelope giving Rosie's return address. She couldn't write to Rosie with no address. Nobody could. They'd just have to wait and hope for Rosie to send another letter.

Marie didn't care so much about Nick as she once had. It was his fault that Rosie had left that September of 1932 and never came home again. The trouble was that Nick probably didn't want Rosie to come back home. If she did, she might want to stay and Nick didn't like Iowa. He liked it out West or down South.

Marie looked out the west window and saw Lars and Lyle drinking water from the old tin cup that hung by the pump. It was the same old cup that she'd pumped water into for Nick when he'd come up into their yard as a dirty, thirsty young tramp. It was then that Marie had learned that the Depression—hard times—had turned many young men into tramps. Nick stayed only half the summer but after he left, so did Rosie, and nothing would ever be the same for the Carlsen family again. Please, God, Marie prayed, take care of Rosie and the baby and Nick too, I guess, and have them come home this summer. Amen.

Would praying do any good? It might, and it was the only thing she could do since her last letter to Rosie had come back marked with the familiar heartbreaking words—moved—address unknown.

When Marie went down the stairs she could hear Lyle and Lars talking to Mamma in the kitchen. When Lyle helped Lars with some work, he always stayed to eat. She wondered what her brother and Lyle would have to say about Trudy. Marie was sure they had noticed her. After all, who wouldn't notice Trudy? What was it she'd yelled at the guy who'd honked at her? Oh, yes—"Look me over, brother! But don't overlook me!" Marie smiled. She'd have to tell Lars and Lyle about that. Trudy had nerve! You had to give her that.

ക 6 ഏ

The Pighouse Roof

MARIE SAT ON THE PIGHOUSE ROOF. THE SUN WAS GOING down. She sat on the pighouse roof because she liked to watch the sun lowering itself into the distant edge of land beyond the fields. She'd been watching sunsets from the pighouse roof since she was a little child after she picked up a basket of pigyard cobs to be burned in the cookstove. It was just something pretty to look at after the grubby job of picking up the black, mud-encrusted cobs and smelling the dirty old pigs that wouldn't get away from her even when she yelled *shoo!*

It was so pretty! The sunset. It wasn't just orange like some pictures artists painted. The sunset from the pighouse roof was hundreds of different colors—pink, lilac, purple, blue-red, blue-gray, and all kinds of dark and pale blues turning into silver behind clouds that blazed into orange and gold around the edges. You could never count all the changing colors in a sunset.

There was also something mysterious about a sunset because of the clouds moving in blue space. You could see figures too, like men marching or kids playing, jumping and running, chasing all kinds of animals. Everything moving, the whole sky on the move, getting ready for darkness. Sunset was a sort of magical time when colors and images in the sky changed so fast you felt if you looked away for even a second you'd miss something.

Marie knew about the inevitable pattern of day sliding into the darkness of night. She was still afraid of darkness but the sunset was kind of like the rainbow. It was like a promise from God that after the dark night, no matter what, the sun would come up in the east just as bright and glorious as it went down in the west.

Marie looked west now. Across the Carlsen fields she could see the trees that shrouded the Clarke farm. She wondered what Bobby Clarke was doing now. Probably milking cows. Marie didn't know him very well because she'd only talked to him once. The Clarkes had only lived across the field for a few months, having moved in in March.

Bobby Clarke was through high school, almost twenty, and Marie thought he looked like Ken Maynard, the handsome dark-haired movie star in the Saturday cowboy movies. "Hi neighbor," he'd smiled at her and given her a ride home in his truck one Saturday when she'd had to walk home from town after confirmation class. Marie had been mad at Lars for not coming after her and making her walk home. Then she stopped caring about that when Bobby Clarke had given her a ride and treated her like she was his age. "Thanks for the ride," she'd said when he stopped the truck by her back door. "Don't mention it," he'd said, "it's a pleasure to have the company of a pretty girl." And Marie had run into the house, no longer mad at Lars, but happy and wondering if Bobby Clarke really thought she looked like the pretty girls in the Ken Maynard movies.

That was the good thing about watching the sunset from the pighouse roof. You could imagine anything you wanted to happen and even pretend that you were beautiful, talented, and rich. The trouble was, you had to come back down to earth, pick up the basket of pigyard cobs; it was still Marie's job to gather them because it was the Depression and coal cost money. And then you had to go back up to the house and realize you were just a plain, ordinary farm girl, not pretty at all, and Bobby Clarke was probably just trying to be nice.

Marie set the basket of cobs down beside the kitchen cookstove. Then she went upstairs to the bathroom to wash her hands and comb her hair. You never knew when Bobby Clarke might come over to see Lars about something or if Lyle Tornquist might come over with Red Gillette. Marie had to admit she liked both Red and Bobby but she might as well be realistic. There wasn't much reason to believe either one of them liked her—at least not that way. Not at all in the romantic way of the moving picture shows. Yet when she looked in the bathroom mirror, she was not always displeased with her image. Some people, Katie Tornquist for instance, said she was growing up to look like Rosie. *"You're getting so pretty, Marie. You remind me so much of Rosie."* Yes, Katie had really said that one day when she'd brought the

Tornquist mail to Katie's kitchen door. Marie didn't know about the looking-like-Rosie part, but she knew she was growing up, not a little kid anymore, and she could look pretty . . . sometimes.

She was a teenager now! Her birthday had been only a few days ago, the eighth of May. Even though the day had marked the difference between childhood and the teens, her birthday had been a disappointment. Of course there had been pink iced cupcakes and strawberry Jell-O at school in the afternoon to celebrate Marie's birthday. Miss Eriksen always brought a treat for each pupil's birthday. That was something every kid at Riverton could depend upon. Mamma had baked a chocolate cake with fudge frosting (Marie's favorite) and put thirteen yellow candles on it. Alfred had sent her a bracelet with charms on it from Chicago. Uncle Chris had come out for supper and had given her a dollar. There were other presents from Mamma and Cora, things like stockings, underwear, and a silk scarf. Karen had given her a snake ring from the dime store.

Nothing came from Rosie. No present. No letter. Not even a birthday card. Marie wasn't mad at Rosie. She was sad. Maybe Rosie didn't have any money to buy even a card or a stamp! Marie went into her bedroom and sat on the cot that had once been Rosie's bed and the longing to be with Rosie made her sad. Marie remembered how good it had been when Rosie and Alfred still lived at home. That time seemed so long ago and even being poor hadn't really been so bad because they'd all been together as a family. She remembered how Alfred used to fight with Mamma because he never had any money. He was the one who had wanted

56

to go to California. Instead he'd gone to Chicago to learn to be an electrician.

It was Rosie who'd gone all the way out to California. She'd gone away with her friend Skinny Fuller; but it was really to find Nick. She married Nick, had the baby, and then they went away from Uncle Jens in Long Beach because Nick wanted to go to Kansas or Texas. The West was so far away and had so many states and cities! Why didn't Rosie write? Of course, Marie knew that Rosie just wasn't a person who liked to write letters. Maybe it made her too homesick. Marie missed her sister so much she felt like crying. But what good would that do? It wouldn't bring Rosie back home. Nothing could do that. Not even praying. You just had to let time go by.

Marie got up off the cot. She'd better go downstairs and help Mamma with supper. Rosie would come home! But she'd take her own sweet time.

Before she left her bedroom, Marie looked out the west window and watched the sun continuing to sink lower behind the pighouse roof. Soon it would be dark and the beautiful colors of sunset would be gone. Marie went downstairs to help Mamma with the work.

✍ 7 ✍

A Lonely Saturday Night

NOW THAT SHE WAS THIRTEEN, MARIE THOUGHT MAMMA should start letting her go to town on Saturday night with Cora and Lars. Trudy Horton had suggested that they could meet at the Rexall Drug Store and go to the moving picture show together. Marie certainly couldn't go with Lars into the pool hall where he met his friends. And of course she wouldn't want to hang around the hardware store with Cora, pretending to buy bolts or nails, while Milton Hayes waited on customers.

Cora wouldn't want Marie around anyway because after almost-bald Milton got done working at ten o'clock, he and Cora would sit in his car on Main Street and act lovey-dovey. Sometimes Marie wished Cora would marry Milton and move uptown. She got so tired of hearing Mamma say, "Well, Cora's twenty-five and you're only thirteen. You can't expect to do the things she does until you're older." One thing she hoped never to do was hang around in a hardware store with somebody like Milton Hayes.

Even if she could, Marie wouldn't want to walk the streets of Spencer alone on Saturday night. Trudy Horton had provided the solution to that problem. She had a friend now to meet uptown and they could go to the movies together. This Saturday night she wouldn't even ask if she could go along to town. She'd just get ready to go and then tell them she was going to meet Trudy. She had over two dollars she'd saved. That was plenty to go to the show and get some ice cream at the drugstore, some popcorn, or something.

After supper, Marie went upstairs and put on her best Sunday dress, green pleated skirt with a white top and green bolero jacket. Mamma had made it from a remnant of green wool she had gotten on sale after Christmas. Marie had picked out the pattern and was satisfied that it was for an older girl of high school age. Also when she wore this dress she had received compliments in Sunday school from some of the most snobbish town girls in her class.

"Where do you think you're going?" asked Lars when she came downstairs in her best dress.

"Uptown," said Marie, "I'm going to the movies with Trudy Horton. I'll call her and she's going to meet me at the drugstore."

Mamma looked at Marie in surprise. "Don't you think you should ask me before you make such plans?"

Marie was ready for this objection.

"Lars never has to ask when he wants to do something."

"He's seventeen," Mamma said, "not thirteen."

"But Lars got to go to town on Saturday night when he was twelve. I remember! You always made Alfred take him!"

"It is different for a boy. You and Trudy are too young to walk the streets on Saturday nights. Nice girls don't do that," said Mamma.

"We aren't going to 'walk the streets,'" Marie cried out. We just want to go to a movie and then I'll wait in the car with Trudy until Lars comes and takes us home. What's wrong with that?"

"I'll tell you what's wrong with it," said Lars. "Trudy Horton *does* walk the streets. She tries to pick up guys. Guys she doesn't know! She's tough. You want people to think you're a girl like that?"

"I don't believe she does that," said Marie. "You just don't want me to go. You get to go to town and that's all you care about. You and Cora both!"

"Mamma's right, Marie," said Cora. "I didn't go uptown and meet my friends for the movies until I started high school. Neither did Rosie. We had to wait until we were older and so will you. Trudy is only fifteen and people talk about her just because her mother never had much sense. I've seen her walking around town at night, but she doesn't know anybody and she is forward and boys are quick to draw conclusions."

"It's not easy to be Trudy. Her mother has allowed her to grow up too fast," said Mamma. "No, you can't go, Marie. You are too young. What Trudy does is her mother's business, not mine. But you are my daughter, Marie, and you will do as your sisters. You may go to town and meet your friends after you start high school."

"Oh, Marie, I'm sorry," Cora cried. "I know how you feel. I've felt the same way when I couldn't do something. Listen, Milton will take you to a movie tomorrow afternoon. It's Sunday and Milton doesn't have to. . . ."

"No!" cried Marie. "No, I don't want to go with you and Milton. I'll just stay home. I'll stay home for the rest of my life!"

Marie turned and ran upstairs to her bedroom and slammed the door. She lay down on her bed and cried and as she did so she heard the squeal of tires on the gravel driveway and knew that her older brother and sister were on their way uptown to enjoy themselves. "I don't care," she said to herself but she knew she was lying. She cared terribly and she kept on crying until Mamma came up the stairs. When she heard her reaching the upper steps, Marie jumped off the cot and rushed into the bathroom and locked the door. Then she turned both faucets on in the sink.

"Marie, I'm sorry. I know it is so sad to be too young."

"I don't care. Spencer's just a small town and it never has any good movies anyway. I'm taking a bath, Mamma."

"All right, Marie," and she heard Mamma go back down the stairs. If she had to stay home, she had to stay home, but she wasn't going to talk to Mamma any more about it. She didn't plan on taking a bath either. Why should she? She wasn't going any place. Marie went back into her bedroom and took off her good dress and put on the one she'd been wearing all day. She was thinking about the extreme boredom of her life when she decided to do something that would give Cora a fit if she knew about it.

Marie went into the room that Cora shared with Karen.

Cora's lipstick, powder, and rouge were on her dresser. Her eyebrow pencil, mascara, and eyelash curler were in a small wooden box by her comb, brush, and hand mirror. Cora was meticulously neat with her possessions and Marie would have to be careful to put everything back in exactly the same place as Cora had left each article. She wouldn't want to risk Cora's outraged fury if she even suspected Marie had touched anything in or on her huge dresser with the only really big mirror in the house.

When they were younger, and not so cautious about concealing the "crime" of using Cora's things, she and Karen played movie star. Karen and Marie spilled powder, left perfume bottles uncorked, and smeared lipstick on the outside of the tube. Cora would be furious and tell Mamma, causing all kinds of problems for them.

Marie put a thick layer of red lipstick on her mouth and rouge on her cheeks, dipped the fluffy puff into pink powder and generously covered her face and neck with it. Then she picked up Cora's eyebrow pencil and made a hard black line over each eye. She went to Cora's closet and picked out a coral-colored silk blouse and put it on over her dress covering it almost entirely.

Marie looked at her image in the large plate glass mirror above Cora's dresser. She looked glamorous! Especially when she combed and brushed her hair off her forehead and behind her ears. Maybe when she was over twenty this was how she'd look! Like a Hollywood starlet or a New York photographer's model. One thing was certain. She wouldn't be staying home on an old farm on Saturday nights. Marie heard a car coming up the driveway.

A Lonely Saturday Night

Looking out the window, Marie saw that it was Uncle Chris in his maroon Model A Ford. When he got out of his car by the pump deck, Marie noticed that he had a white paper sack in his hand. Marie could guess what was in it— orange slices, or lemon drops, or *peanut clusters!* Whenever he came out on Saturday nights to visit with Mamma, Uncle Chris, who was a bachelor, always stopped at the Candy Kitchen and bought candy for Marie and Karen. Marie hoped he'd bought peanut clusters this time. There might not be as many, but they were better than orange slices or lemon drops. Marie hurriedly put Cora's things back in their rightful place, and washed and combed herself back to normal.

Mamma and Karen were standing beside Uncle Chris near his car when Marie came outside. Karen handed Marie the white paper sack. Thank goodness! It *was* peanut clusters! And a lot of them, a very big sackful! Karen was chewing a piece of candy and reaching for another. Uncle Chris smiled at them. Sometimes Marie did not mind so much that Uncle Chris still thought she was a little kid like Karen when it meant getting plenty of candy.

"Come, it's not dark yet, Hannah," said Uncle Chris. "If you are too tired, as you say, to go to town, let us at least go for a ride. Come, get in the car, Marie and Karen."

They went for a very long ride south along Highway 71 and they drove through the main streets of little towns. All the stores were open and there were people walking around because it was Saturday night. Marie wished they would stop in a town and have a milkshake or something but she knew that Uncle Chris and Mamma, being from Denmark, were both far too old-fashioned to do anything like that.

When they drove past farms in the countryside, she and Karen counted white horses to see who could get the most. Whoever said *white horse* first got it. They did this until it was too dark to do it anymore. Uncle Chris and Mamma talked in the front seat while from the back seat windows Karen and Marie watched the fleeting lights of farm buildings along the highway. The trouble with living on farms, Marie thought, was that your neighbors lived so far away. You had to walk so far to visit anybody. How wonderful it would be to live in town where neighbors lived with backyards side by side. No, she would never live on a farm when she got married. She'd even rather be a missionary in China and stay single like that pretty woman who had once visited her Sunday school class.

On the ride back home, Karen curled up and went to sleep. Marie managed to put her legs up on the seat and lean back in a comfortable position but she couldn't sleep. She watched the moon, which seemed to be following along with the car in the dark night sky. She'd learned in science that the moon was closer to the earth than the sun but that seemed strange. The sun looked close. The moon seemed so far away. Someday, if she ever went to college—as Mamma hoped she would because she said Marie was the smartest, trying to make her feel good because she wasn't the prettiest— if she ever went to college maybe she would study astronomy and learn all about the universe. But then again. . . .

"There's not a peep back there," Mamma said. "They must have both fallen asleep."

"They are so young. They have no worries," said Uncle Chris, "Sleep comes easy to them."

Marie did not tell them she was still awake. She would rather just think about things than have to talk to them.

She couldn't help hearing their usual conversations about crops, bank loans, and the price of corn and pigs. Nothing they talked about interested her until they started talking about Alfred and Rosie.

"I worry so about them," said Mamma. "Alfred is almost finished with his electrician course now but he says there are no jobs in Chicago, not even for the experienced electricians. Many of *them* have been laid off. Cousin Dagmar called me from Chicago. Alfred still lives in the rooming house and he visits with her and Hans and their children sometimes on Sundays. Dagmar asked me if Alfred had written that he might go out to Montana with some people he knows who say they are building dams out West and there is work for electricians. He has mentioned such things in his letters but I do not want him to go out where he cannot even be sure there will be a job for him when he gets there. I do not want Alfred bumming around looking for work."

"He cannot be tied to your apron strings, Hannah. He is over twenty-six years old. He must decide for himself what he must do. When you sent him off to be an electrician, you must have known he would not come back to the farm like a whipped dog. He was a boy when he left. He did what you asked him to do. We have talked before about that. A boy cannot grow into a man until he is able to use his own judgment and make his own decisions. Alfred will do what he must, like all other men."

Marie thought about Alfred going out West to Montana. That meant it would be a long time until he would come home again. She missed Alfred too, although not nearly as much as she missed Rosie.

"Yes, I suppose you are right about Alfred," Mamma mused after a silence. "He never liked farming and he became so restless, so discontented, and then he became bitter and began to brood and hate. I was afraid he would do something against the law and land in jail. You are right, Christian. Alfred must decide what he will do. It is just that he is still young, and he could go hungry off on his own. If he goes out West, I cannot help it, but I will have so many fears for him."

"I am sure *Mor* and *Far* had fears for us when we crossed the Atlantic, nay? But we would not listen to their fears. Can't you see it is the same with Alfred?"

"Yes, I know," said Mamma. "I know now what it must have been like for them to lose us for they must have known we would not be back. But at least in 1901 we had Soren to come to in Iowa. They knew then we would be safe with our older brother. It is different for Alfred. The times are not the same. Alfred wants to go off and look for work among strangers and that is different."

"It might have been better for me if I had gone off among strangers," said Uncle Chris. "I depended too much upon Soren and he still, even now at my age, thinks he should tell me what to do. I listened too much to Soren when I would have been better off to trust my own judgment. But that is water over the dam now and I cannot blame Soren. I can only blame myself."

Marie did not understand what Uncle Chris meant by that. Uncle Soren never told people what to do. Tante Karen was the bossy one, not Uncle Soren. Then she remembered what Mamma had said about her and Trudy helping Tante Karen clean her cottage at the lake after school was out in June. It would be fun to go to Arnold's Park, an amusement place with carnival rides and everything, and go swimming with Trudy Horton . . . if, and that was the big if, if Tante Karen would let them stop working long enough to do things that were fun. Marie made up her mind. It would be better to go to the cottage at the lake with Trudy than to stay home and do nothing but dishes, cleaning, and farm chores. She'd go. At least life was never boring around Trudy!

Now they were talking about Rosie and Mamma's worries about her. Well, Marie knew all about that.

"We have no idea where she is or how they are getting along. It has been over four months since we have heard from Rose."

"Give her time. If things were going too bad, you would hear. She will write. Give her time," said Uncle Chris.

"Yes, I suppose she is all right. Time goes by so fast and there is so much to do when you are married and have a husband and child. I did not write to *Mor* and *Far* as often as I should have. Yes, Rose is probably just fine.". . . Mamma's voice trailed off sadly. A moment later, she asked, more briskly, "Have you heard from Andreas in Denmark, Christian?"

Now they began talking about their brother, Uncle Andreas, and all the other relatives who still lived in Denmark. They talked about Germany and a man named Hitler who was building up a great army and had said in a book that Germany should rule the world. "They are worried about him in Denmark. They are afraid he cannot be stopped and there will be danger to all of Europe." Uncle Chris went on to say that many of his friends who had not left Denmark now wished they had gone to America when they were young. "Andreas says it may not be safe much longer to live in the old country. They are afraid, Hannah, afraid of war and Denmark is not prepared for war."

The voices in the front seat droned on, talking about places, people, and times Marie knew nothing about. Marie continued to watch the moon still following outside the car along Highway 71. Finally she fell asleep to the singsong sound of the car motor and the quiet voices in the front seat.

Somebody shook her shoulder. "Wake up, Marie," said Uncle Chris, "we are home. Can you wake up enough to walk into the house? I will carry Karen, Hannah."

Uncle Chris carried Karen into Mamma's bedroom and put her on the bed. Karen did not wake up. Marie followed and sleepily climbed up on the bed beside Karen.

Marie went back to sleep, but not before she heard Mamma say. "How nice that they, at least, are not old enough to have large fears and worries. Come, Christian, I will make us a pot of coffee and we will visit until Lars and Cora come home from town." From her sleepy haze, Marie wondered: How could Mamma be so wrong? How could she be so sure Marie had no large fears and worries?

❧ 8 ❧

Marie Loses a Bet

MARIE AND LYLE WERE WALKING ALONG HIGHWAY 71 TOward their homes. Violets and daisies were growing in the ditches now. Marie had gathered a bouquet of flowers for Mamma and Lyle had picked some for his mother too. That was the nice thing about Lyle. Unlike most farm boys, he didn't see anything sissy about picking flowers or talking about how blue the sky was and how nice the green grass made everything look. She could talk to Lyle about all kinds of things and he never acted like she was stupid just because she was a girl.

"Lyle, have you decided what poem you're going to say for an oration when you graduate from eighth grade?"

"Sure," laughed Lyle. "I've already got it memorized. Want to hear it?"

"Yes, if you want to recite it."

"The boy sat on the burning deck, eating peanuts by the peck," Lyle said in a loud voice.

"Lyle, I'm serious. It's almost time for the township picnic and you have to say a poem when you graduate from eighth grade. Everybody has to recite a poem or make some kind of speech when they graduate. So which are you going to do, recite a poem or give a speech?"

"Neither," said Lyle. "I'm not going to give a speech and I'm not going to stand on the stage and say a long-winded poem that nobody even wants to have to listen to."

"Lyle, you'll *have* to. You know that!"

"Well, I won't! Want to bet on it?"

"How much? And you better have it because you won't win," said Marie, considering that it would be a very safe bet for her to make; and she still did have a dollar—the one Uncle Chris had given her for her thirteenth birthday had not been spent. It would be nice to have two dollars instead of just one. "Have you got a dollar to bet, Lyle?"

"Sure," he said. "I don't make bets if I can't back them up. Let's shake hands on it."

Marie knew Lyle could be stubborn but she also knew Katie Tornquist, his mother, and Miss Eriksen, their teacher. No matter how much he wanted to, Marie was sure Lyle could not get out of a recitation or an oration on the day of his graduation. Miss Eriksen and Katie would make sure that he did what he was expected to do and not disgrace them. Marie was so confident of winning that she even began thinking of the many things one could buy with as much as two dollars.

"Last time I saw Red Gillette, he asked if I thought you'd run in the seventh and eighth grade boys and girls foot races. He says you haven't got a chance of winning against

70

him this year. He never got over losing the race to you when he was in sixth and you were in fifth. I don't think you could win this year, Marie, so you might as well not try."

"Well, I haven't even decided if I want to be in the races," Marie said. "There's nothing so great about winning a quarter for a race. It's kind of childish anyway." Marie wasn't sure if she should plan to compete. Cora had gotten unusually generous and had bought her a yellow organdy dress that Marie had found marked down to three dollars in The Beehive bargain basement. Marie planned to wear the new dress to the township picnic and didn't want to get hot and sticky running the race.

Marie did not run in the races the day of the township picnic, but neither did Red Gillette. He sat on the eighth grade graduation platform with about a dozen Riverton Township graduates. He wore a dark suit with a white carnation in the lapel, and a red tie that matched his red hair. His voice was loud and clear.

> Thou too sail on, oh ship of state,
> Sail on, oh union, proud and great

With great confidence and eloquence Red recited the patriotic poem. His voice boomed out over the audience, as he delivered the many verses of the long poem, making every fiber of Marie's body thrill with pride because she was an American.

Much as Marie would have liked to be through with country school and up on that stage with the eighth grade graduates, she was also glad that today was not the day that she would have to stand alone in the middle of the stage and recite a poem in front of an audience that was made up of the whole township. There were ten school districts, each with its own small country school, in the township. This was the supreme test of an eighth grade graduate—to prove that he or she, beyond passing written exams, could master the skill of public speaking or dramatic elocution.

Other boys and girls came forward to present themselves to the audience, were introduced by their teachers, and then left to stand alone center stage and perform. Marie sympathized with a boy who shifted from one foot to the other and mumbled Edgar Guest's "It Takes a Heap of Livin' to Make a House a Home" poem down into his shirt collar. She felt sorry for a tall, thin girl who was visibly trembling as she recited a poem in a voice no louder than a whisper. Good or bad, the audience applauded loudly for each performance as the graduate, clutching the hard-won diploma, returned to be seated in the row of folding chairs, the seats of honor.

As moving and memorable as Red Gillette's deliverance of his graduation oration had been, it was not the best performance. Lyle Tornquist stole the show! Lyle, who liked to be different from everybody else, sang a song. It was a special surprise because whenever anybody at school had asked him which poem he had chosen to recite, he'd always just laughed and said, "The boy stood on the burning deck, eating peanuts by the peck!"

So on the day he graduated from eighth grade and sat on the stage with his legs crossed, neat as a pin in his new blue suit, and wearing his big dimpled smile, Marie was astonished to hear Lyle announce he was going to sing!

Lyle told the audience that "America the Beautiful" was written by a woman, Katharine Lee Bates, who was born in 1859 and died in 1929. Miss Eriksen sat down at the piano and played the introduction and Lyle sang all four verses. When Lyle sat down, the audience seemed never to want to stop applauding. Marie thought she knew why Lyle Tornquist had chosen to sing. He'd bet her a dollar and he'd also told everyone in school he'd bet each of them a quarter that nobody could make him recite a poem when he graduated from eighth grade. Besides that, Lyle had apparently figured a way out of having to memorize one. Marie knew Lyle had a terrible memory. But he did have a good voice!

Marie was sitting by Trudy Horton in the audience. Trudy had come out for the little white kitten but refused to take it home with her when Marie told her that Karen really didn't want to give it up. "Shoot! Don't make no never mind to me which one I get. If you feel partial to the white kitten, you keep it and give me whichever one you want me to take." So Karen had given Trudy a little gray kitten and Trudy, cuddling the kitten in her arms, had said, "I'm just as tickled with this one, Karen Kiddie."

So of course, Karen had told Trudy all about the township picnic which would be held the day after country schools were let out for the summer. "You want to go with us, Trudy? You can if you want to because it's for everybody in the township and even though you live in Spencer, you live in Riverton Township too!" It was arranged that the Carlsens would take Trudy to the picnic.

"Oh God," said Trudy now with her handkerchief at her eyes, "I never heard anybody sing so beautiful in my

73

life. I can't help bawling, Marie, Lyle sung so damn beautiful."

Of course, the next day, Lyle came over to collect his bet from Marie. Marie felt sad to say good-bye to the dreams she had of spending Lyle's dollar, not to mention her own. If only she'd given a try to running the foot race. Then at least she'd have won a quarter. Now she'd have no money at all. She should have known she couldn't outwit Lyle, who'd obviously had something up his sleeve the whole time.

Marie's biggest secret, though, was that she felt sad not only about losing the bet, but because Red Gillette had graduated from eighth grade too. Now he had somehow become a person of maturity and Marie was sure she was beneath his notice. With no money and another dull summer ahead of her, Marie took refuge in romantic novels to make life more interesting. Some of these had been left behind by Rosie and these were always the ones Marie especially liked, because Rosie had read them first, years ago. Sometimes, in Marie's daydreams, the heroes of these books looked like Red Gillette. Sometimes they looked like their handsome older neighbor, Bobby Clarke. But more often they looked like the actor, Ken Maynard. However they looked, the heroine was always Marie, though she wouldn't have told anyone that for the world.

Soon after the picnic, Marie received a long letter from Rosie! It made up for all the months that she had worried about her sister's whereabouts. The letter was full of news. She and Nick were working on a ranch in Kansas. They had a little tenant house and Nick did farm work and Rosie did housework. There was an address to which they could write and Rosie said they were well and happy. There were pictures of blond, curly-haired Tommy. He was a darling baby and Rosie said he was very good.

After Marie read the letter, she gave it to Mamma. Mamma looked at the baby's pictures for a long time.

"So this is a picture of my first grandchild," she said. "He is getting to be a big boy. Soon he will be grown up too. What will life be like for him? He looks like his father, but let us hope he may grow up without such a scar."

Marie remembered Nick's handsome young face with the ugly red scar. He'd told Alfred it was from a cut left by a knife used by men who had accused him of stealing a dollar in a hobo jungle. She remembered how Mamma had said that the scar on Nick's face had healed but the scar on his mind had not. Marie wondered if Nick was happy now with Rosie and the baby and if he'd be content to settle down and stop moving from place to place. She hoped so because then they'd always know where Rosie was living and wouldn't have to worry about her so much. Anyway, the letter sounded like Rosie was okay. It had ended: "Marie, write to me again soon. We're getting along just fine and it shouldn't be long before we'll be able to come home and see everyone. Write and tell me what's going on. Love you forever, Rosie."

That night, after she had read Rosie's letter over at least a dozen times and decided that in the picture baby Tommy did look like Nick, only without the scar, Marie watched the sun going down behind the pighouse roof. She watched while sitting on the cot and looking out the west window of her room. What was Kansas like? She imagined that it was probably a lot like Iowa except with fields of wheat instead of corn. Kansas is a lot closer than California, Marie thought, and that meant Rosie was closer to home.

Waiting for Rosie, Nick, and the baby wouldn't be so hard now anyway because summer vacation had started. There was one flaw in Marie's happiness. Ethel Jorth and her family had moved back to Omaha because her father had gotten a better job there. She missed Ethel in confirmation class. The other girls were not much fun and the boys were okay but they just talked to each other.

But there was Trudy Horton! Now on Saturdays, since Ethel had moved away, after confirmation class was over, Marie did not want to wait alone at the Rexall Drug Store for Lars to pick her up and take her home. Instead she walked to Trudy's house at the edge of town. She always had fun with Trudy!

Now that Marie had Rosie's address, Marie could write and tell her what was going on at home. Nothing was going on! Unless you wanted to count the news that Magnus was finished going to Grandview College in Des Moines and now knew English. Since Rosie had never known Magnus maybe she wouldn't be interested in him. Marie certainly wasn't going to write about all the boring things that happened on a farm! Or about the township picnic or going to confirmation class and how much she disliked the preacher. That wouldn't be news to Rosie. She *did* write almost a page about Trudy. She thought Rosie would like Trudy. Then she did think of some more possible news. Cora and Milton might (just might) get married before the end of summer, maybe in July. If they did, Cora would move to Everly and live in town there in a little house that belonged to Milton's parents.

Yes, news about Cora and Milton finally tying the knot (Marie decided to use that expression) would really be news to Rosie. Then she could write about Alfred thinking about going out to Montana with some friends to see if they could find work as electricians on the big dam the government was building. Wasn't Montana pretty close to Kansas? Maybe Alfred could visit Rosie. She'd really be happy if something like that could happen. Writing to Rosie made Marie feel close to her. "Write soon—Love, Marie," she signed her letter. Then she folded the letter, put it in an envelope, addressed it, and asked Cora to get a three-cent stamp for it and put it in the mail when she went to town.

Surely it wouldn't be long now (since they were as close to home as Kansas) that Rosie, Nick, and the baby would just come up the driveway, walk in the back door, and into the kitchen, and surprise everybody. *"Hey! We're home!"* Rosie would probably yell and the whole family would gather around. What a wonderful day that was going to be!

Tante Karen did have Marie and Trudy Horton spend a few days with her at the lake to help clean her summer cottage. It was not really much of a vacation because Tante Karen made them scrub floors, wash windows, and air out musty old bedding that had been stored through the winter. Amazingly, Tante Karen, who was never known for her generosity, gave them each a dollar for helping her.

They spent their money in the fun house at the Arnold's Park amusement carnival at Lake Okoboji and on candy and pop. When their money was gone, they went to the beach at Terrace Park. Marie almost drowned! Trudy was a good swimmer and swam out to the raft which was in water above their heads. Marie could float but she couldn't swim very well. She tried to follow Trudy out to the raft but she couldn't make it. As she thrashed around under water, her lungs filling up with water, Marie thought—*so this is it! I'm only thirteen and I'm going to drown! I'm going to die! Please, God, don't let me die now when I'm only thirteen!*

Suddenly somebody was pulling her through the water. She learned later that it was Trudy. A man on the beach gave her artificial respiration and Marie felt like she'd never get through coughing up water. "She'll be okay but she had a close call," said the man. "Don't go out in water above your head until you learn to swim," he told Marie.

Trudy made her sit by a tree with a blanket somebody had put around her until she was rested enough to walk back to Tante Karen's summer cottage.

"Don't ever tell anybody I almost drowned," Marie said to Trudy. "You saved my life. It's an awful feeling when you think you're going to die." Trudy promised not to tell.

Tante Karen was mad because she was packed and ready to take them back to the farm. The summer cottage was clean and she said they'd certainly spent enough time at the park and in the lake. "You said a mouthful," said Trudy and in spite of everything, Marie had to laugh.

❧ 9 ❧

Not Easy to Be Trudy

SATURDAY WAS KIDDIE DAY IN BOTH THE MOVIE HOUSES IN Spencer. That meant that any kid under sixteen could get into the moving picture show for a nickel. For Marie and Karen, Saturday afternoons that summer of 1934 were spent going to the movies with Trudy Horton. Trudy would be sixteen in September so her Saturdays to pass for "a kiddie" at the box office were numbered.

Sometimes there were double features, two full-length movies, one a regular motion picture featuring such stars as Jean Harlowe, Joan Crawford, Ginger Rogers and Fred Astaire, or other big box-office attractions; and also a companion film that was a cowboy movie with Marie's idol, Ken Maynard, or such movie stars as Tim McCoy, Hoot Gibson, or Gene Autry. Trudy Horton's house at the edge of town was a convenient stopping off place when they walked to and from town.

So, in spite of her tough ways Trudy Horton, the kid from town, became their closest friend and companion.

After the Saturday movies, Marie and Karen would walk with Trudy along the old gravel road to Trudy's house on the southern outskirts of town. They might stay at Trudy's for awhile and Erma would give them something good to eat—a snack of cake, pie, cookies, or strawberry Jell-O topped with whipped cream. One of Trudy's mother's great pleasures in life was baking and eating and urging others to eat what she baked to gain weight. "Sit down! Eat! You're both thin as rails. It's not healthy to be so skinny!" Erma would urge Marie and Karen to keep eating.

Marie understood now why both Erma and Trudy were fat. The aroma of something in the oven or on the stove filled the house and it was always delicious. Beauty had supplied milk and cream until she went dry and before she came fresh again, Marie and Karen brought dairy products from the farm. Mamma even gave Erma lard, butter, frying chickens, fruits, and vegetables. "You feed my children so often, it is no more than right that they bring something for you to cook and bake with. We have plenty of food on the farm and the prices they charge in the stores are too high. You are so good to Marie and Karen, it is the least I can do for you," Mamma told Trudy's mother and she always refused to take any money from her.

Old Jake was not fat. He was probably about fifty years old and his long thin face usually had a stubble of gray whiskers, his watery blue eyes were often bloodshot, and he always needed a haircut. He tried to be friendly but Marie felt uncomfortable around him. There was something strange about the way he looked at her. Once at the kitchen table, he and Marie happened to be sitting alone and he had put his face very close to hers and said she smelled sweet as a rose. Marie had left the table quickly. Old Jake's breath smelled awful, like cigarettes and whiskey—putrid and rotten. Marie could understand why Trudy didn't like him and never talked to him. He was nuts all right!

There was the time Marie and Karen had stayed overnight with Trudy and she'd gone with them to Sunday school at the Danish Lutheran Church. She and Karen had stopped to get their clothes afterward before walking the two miles home to the farm. She would never forget the violence of that morning after Sunday school when the three of them, she, Karen, and Trudy, stood at the kitchen door, afraid to enter. Old Jake was yelling at Trudy's mother while she was plucking a chicken at the sink. Suddenly, she turned and threw the half-plucked chicken at old Jake's head. He ducked and the chicken hit the wall and dropped to the floor. Then Trudy's mother picked up the pan with the feathers and threw that at old Jake. In a matter of seconds, old Jake was across the room, choking Trudy's mother, both hands around her neck shaking her. "Some day, Erma! Some day, by God! You will cause me to kill you!"

Then he saw them standing in the kitchen doorway. He dropped his hands from the woman's neck and although her face looked wild and her eyes were bulging, she seemed to be all right.

"Get out of here! Damn you kids! Get out of this house!" Jake shouted.

They ran then. The three of them ran until they got to

the small woods at the edge of the acreage. Then Trudy stopped. She was crying. "Go home, Marie and Karen. I'll bring your clothes out to you. Don't worry about that."

"Trudy, don't stay here," said Karen. "Come home with us now. He might kill you too."

"No, he won't," said Trudy in her gruff boylike voice. "He won't kill Ma and he won't kill me. He's too chicken! But if I don't get old enough to leave home pretty soon, I might kill him! Go on home. I'll be okay. So will Ma. We're used to him."

Of course Karen told Mamma what happened. Karen always told Mamma everything that happened, good or bad. Mamma was angry. She'd already heard about the red and blue welts on Trudy's thighs after old Jake had whipped her with his belt.

"That devil," Mamma said. "That good-for-nothing devil! I don't understand what Erma ever saw in him or why she lives with that devil. She should get rid of him! It is her home, willed to her by the old Hortons because she was their only child. They were good people. It is so sad that she ever settled for such a devil!"

Marie understood now why Trudy was so tough. She had to be tough! Marie was afraid that Mamma would not let them walk home with Trudy after Karen had told her what had happened. But Mamma just felt sorry for Trudy. "You tell her she can come home with you when there is trouble at home. She has no brothers or sisters or relatives. It is not easy to be Trudy Horton. Tell her she is always welcome here and that I want her to feel at home with us. I was a good friend of her grandmother's before she died and

I know how she worried about Trudy. Gertrude was a good friend and a wonderful woman. It is too bad for Trudy that she is gone."

After that, Trudy Horton became almost another addition to the family, another plate at the table. She idolized Mrs. Carlsen and Trudy worked hard to help her whether it was cooking, cleaning, working in the vegetable garden, or any other farm chore. They talked and laughed as they worked together. It gave Marie more time to read. Marie wondered if having Trudy around helped Mamma keep from missing Rosie so much. It was almost as if Trudy took Rosie's place at the table and filled an empty spot in Mamma's heart. But of course she could not really take Rosie's place. Nobody could ever do that!

৩৪ 10 ৯৬

Penny Auctions

THAT SUMMER OF 1934 THE EVENINGS WERE HOT AND LONG. It stayed light a long time after chores were done and there was nothing to do in the house except read or listen to the radio.

Marie was bored at night. So was Lars. The Tornquists had driven over and picked up Mamma and taken her with them to a meeting for farmers at the school grounds. Cora and Karen were upstairs and Marie and Lars were alone downstairs.

"Come on, Marie," said Lars. "Let's go up to the meeting and see what it's all about."

"Mamma doesn't want us to go," said Marie. "She might get mad. She says it's a meeting just for adults, not for school kids."

"I'm in high school and I get sick of her telling me what

I can do and what I can't. Anyway, there'll be so many people there, she won't even see us. Cora and Karen will just think we went outside someplace. Come on, Marie. We can walk through the cornfield along the highway and nobody will even notice where we're going. I want to see what's going on."

Marie was pleased that Lars wanted her to go with him. It was not often that he treated her as an equal. She wasn't quite sure why he was doing so now but she suspected that he had a reason. Maybe he's lonely too she thought.

"Okay," she said because she'd heard there might be more than a hundred people at the meeting and that would be something to see. It was certainly better to go with Lars than to stay home with Cora and Karen and do nothing.

As they walked along Highway 71, inside the fence of their own cornfield, Lars had plenty to complain about. He was mad at Mamma, so mad that he couldn't tell anybody outside the family, and now Marie knew why he'd asked her to go with him. If you didn't tell somebody how mad you were, you just couldn't stand it. Marie realized that she was the only person he could talk to about family things that griped him and she might even sympathize with his feelings of frustration.

"Treats me just like a little kid, like I don't know anything! Lyle and Norman Tornquist and a lot of guys my age will be there. Ma said, 'No, Lars, I don't want you to get mixed up in all this farm trouble. I had enough of that with Alfred.' Well, I'm not Alfred and I wouldn't do anything stupid like blocking the highway and talking about breaking the law like he did!"

Marie remembered how Alfred used to argue with Mamma about selling the farm because they never had any money to buy things they needed and how he was working his butt off and couldn't even make enough for pocket money. She remembered how Alfred had joined the farmers' union and helped plan strikes and how Mamma would sit up late at night, drinking black coffee, and worrying about whether or not Alfred would come home or whether he was in jail with other farmers who caused trouble.

Marie didn't want to talk to Lars about Alfred. Lars was too mad at Mamma to even think straight. She just let Lars go on complaining.

"Sure. Alfred was a big shot! A big wheel farm union guy and he was always telling Ma what she should do. I never tell her what to do. I always do just what she says, and I'm getting sick of being bossed around and treated like a little kid just because Alfred's going on thirty now and going to be a big-shot electrician in Chicago. Can't find a job even after he got through the trade school. That's how smart old Alfred is!"

"It's not his fault, Lars," said Marie. "It's still the Depression and jobs are hard to find, even in Chicago. Cousin Dagmar said so when she talked to Mamma on the phone. That's why Rosie and Nick have to travel all over, isn't it? Anyway, Alfred might go out West and work on a dam the government's building and then maybe he'll go to Kansas and see Rosie and they might both come back home and. . . ."

"Alfred's always full of hot air. If he can't find a job in Chicago, he won't find one out West either," said Lars.

There was no use talking to Lars. He was too mad. They

Penny Auctions

walked along, inside their fence, until they reached the schoolhouse corner which was only a half mile from their house.
By the schoolyard, along the dirt road, the gravel road, and
even along Highway 71, cars and trucks were parked. There
were even more vehicles parked in the schoolyard. Crowds
of people, mainly men and older boys, though there were a
few women among them, were standing around listening to
a man giving a speech from the back of a truck. He was
talking very loudly but they couldn't hear what he was saying.
    "I'm going over and see what's going on," said Lars.
"Ma won't see me in the crowd."
    "I want to go too," said Marie.
    "Okay, but then you'll be in trouble with Ma too if we
get caught."
    "I don't care," said Marie.
    Most of the speeches were over, but the men were still
asking questions and talking. They found Lyle among all the
strangers.
    "What did they decide to do?" asked Lars.
    "Hold penny auctions like they've done in Minnesota.
These guys are here telling how to do it," said Lyle. "It's a
way to keep the bank from taking everything away from farmers
when the stuff they own—like machinery and livestock—gets
sold at farm auctions to pay off bank loans."
    "How's it work, Lyle?" asked Lars.
    "Well, take us, for example. They got a farm sale lined
up to sell off all our machinery, livestock, and house stuff.
Dad wanted more time to pay and the bank won't give it to
him. So when they hold the farm sale, a hundred or more
farmers will crowd around the auctioneer. They'll start the

87

bidding with one penny and that's why they're called penny auctions. If anybody comes to our farm sale and tries to bid over a dime for anything we got, the farmers will warn him that they'll break his skull!"

"You mean then that the bank will only get a few pennies for your Angus bull if that's all anybody bids? Is that legal, Lyle?" asked Lars.

"Sure it's legal," said Lyle. "It'll be open bidding just like at any other farm auction except that everybody will pay cash and get a bill of sale on the spot. Then the next day, instead of taking home what they bought for pennies, a nickel, or a dime, they just give it back to my dad. The bank gets the proceeds from the auction but it will be like chicken feed compared to how much money a regular auction brings in. At the penny auctions, they start bidding at a penny and that's as high as a lot of stuff is going to go. The next day everything that's been sold is given back to the farmer and there's no law in this country that says you can't give away something you've bought and paid for."

"That's smart," said Lars. "I wonder who ever thought up an idea like that."

"Nobody around here," said Lyle. "It might even have been a college professor or somebody. Who cares who figured it out as long as it works."

Marie asked, "If you don't have to let the bank sell everything and take the money, then you won't have to move, will you, Lyle?" Katie had told Mamma that the Tornquist family was going to move to town because farming was too hard a way to make a living.

"We'll move to town this summer anyway," said Lyle

sadly. "Ma doesn't like living on a farm anymore. She even thinks John Dillinger, Baby Face Nelson, Pretty Boy Floyd, or somebody is going to be running around loose and drive in our yard and kill us some night when my dad's not home. She calls them desperadoes and she's scared to death that the whole country is turning into gangsters and outlaws. She wants to move to town so I guess we will."

A few weeks later the Tornquist farm sale was held. Farmers began arriving very early and, just as Lyle had predicted, the crowd was enormous. Mamma went and to their surprise, she not only allowed Lars to go, but said Marie and Karen could go. Katie Tornquist's household furniture was also to be auctioned. Mamma said there would be no trouble as nobody except farmers would try to bid. Marie went out by the Tornquist barn to watch the auctioning off of the livestock.

"What am I bid for this steer?" bawled the auctioneer.

"One cent!" called a loud voice.

"Let's not be ridiculous," yelled the auctioneer. "Do I hear a starting bid of a dollar?"

Stony silence met the auctioneer's urging to bid higher. He finally had to let the steer go for three cents. Marie watched a man come forward and get the bill of sale for three pennies. It was plain the bank was not going to get much money by selling Mr. Tornquist's equipment, animals, or grain; but it was too late to call off the auction. From the standpoint of the farmers, the penny auction had succeeded. Katie had Lyle, Norman, and Lars carry her furniture back inside the house. Each table, bed, or chair—everything—had been auctioned off for a few pennies and nobody, man or woman, who won the bid wanted to take away anything that belonged to Katie Tornquist.

It was not long after the Tornquist farm auction, that they moved to town. Mr. Tornquist had found a job as an assistant to the county agricultural agent. It was hard for Marie to imagine another family living across Highway 71 in the house that had always been the Tornquist home. For a little while, she hoped that some people would move in with a girl her age. That hope was soon dashed.

"Guess who our new neighbor is going to be? Henry Byers! Henry wanted a place of his own and Max decided to set him up in farming on the Tornquist place. Max Byers is the only farmer around here with enough cash to buy everything from Lyle's dad and rent the farm," said Lars. "Henry's lucky he's got a rich old man. If he lives to be ninety, he'll never be anything but a big spoiled baby, too stupid and lazy to do anything."

Marie had to agree with Lars on the matter of Henry Byers. Nobody would want a jerk like Henry for a close neighbor. But, Marie thought sadly, it looked like they were stuck with him.

❧ 11 ❧

Fourth of July Shivaree

"I CAN'T BELIEVE IT," SAID MARIE. "YOU MEAN CORA'S GETTING married the fourth of July and She doesn't even get to have a wedding?"

Mamma sighed. "Marie, you are old enough to understand that there is not enough money to pay for a church wedding. Cora realizes that these are hard times. We cannot afford all the expense—invitations, wedding gown, flowers from a florist, a big reception. Cora and Milton are quite happy to be married in Reverend Norgaard's parsonage with two of their friends as witnesses. You have no reason to complain, Marie."

"How are they going to get any presents if they don't have a wedding? That's stupid. Other people have weddings in a church and I'll bet some of them live on farms and are just as poor as we are."

"We are not *other people*," said Mamma. "Cora and Milton

will have a nice ceremony at the minister's house and afterward, we will have a wedding dinner here at home for them.

Trudy was sitting at the kitchen table with Marie and Mrs. Carlsen. They were snapping the ends off of green beans, preparing them for canning. A bushel of beans, recently picked from the garden, was by the table. Marie hated green beans. Mamma would can over fifty quarts and they would be eating them all winter. With Trudy's help this June, it was easier to pick and get them ready to be canned. Trudy liked to work at the Carlsen farm. She said it reminded her of when they lived on the farm over by Royal before the bank foreclosed on old Jake and they had to move to the acreage near town.

"Who's going to be at the dinner here?" asked Marie.

"The wedding couple, their witnesses, Reverend Norgaard and his wife, and just our own family. We'll pull out the dining-room table to seat twelve, use the linen tablecloth, the good dishes and silverware, and the crystal drinking goblets from the china closet. We'll have fried chicken and mashed potatoes. Apple pie and ice cream. It will be nice, Marie. You'll see." Mamma smiled at Trudy. "Of course you will be here too, Trudy. You are like part of the family."

Trudy had a speculative look on her face. It was unusual for her to remain quiet for so long when something as important as Cora's approaching marriage was being discussed.

"Boy, have I got an idea," she exclaimed now. "Listen, let me tell you what they did over at Royal when people got married. They had a shivaree! That's what. A rip snortin' kettle bangin' shivaree. Everybody came! Even people from other towns who never even laid eyes on the bride and groom until the night of the shivaree. Boy, oh boy, would they ever get the presents. They even got chairs, tables, and beds. One

couple even got an icebox. You can't even imagine how much
stuff a couple can get off of a shivaree."

"Trudy, I don't think Cora and Milton would want that
kind of attention when they get married. They just want a
quiet simple ceremony without any fuss or bother," said
Mamma.

"Shoot!" said Trudy, "there's no fuss or bother to it.
It's all a surprise celebration. They don't get to know a thing
about it until all the hooting and hollering starts up and people
start driving up into the yard with the food and drinks and
start unloading the presents. Boy, there's nothing more fun
than a good old-fashioned shivaree."

"Well, we did have marriage celebrations such as that
and invited friends and neighbors back in the old country.
Sometimes they lasted until morning with people eating, drinking, dancing, and celebrating with the bride and groom. Yes,
I can remember how back in the old country a marriage was
a big occasion and—"

"It should be," said Trudy, "even in a depression. We
could have a hard-times barn dance. We'd do it all, wouldn't
we, Marie, and. . . ."

"Now, Trudy, we have to think about this," said Mamma.
"I don't know if Cora and Milton would—"

"They don't get to have a thing to say about it," said
Trudy. "That's the whole idea. A surprise! It's like a wonderful
wedding surprise that they'll remember the rest of their lives
and they deserve it! Believe me, Cora and Milton both work
hard, her teaching and him clerking in that hardware store
and getting low pay and no thanks. Cora and Milton deserve
to have one night of fun out of their hard lives."

Marie noticed a small smile playing around the corners

of Mamma's lips. It was pretty hard for anybody not to get amused about Trudy's enthusiasm. It was fun to think of a wild and noisy celebration for prim and proper Cora and boring old Milton. Marie could tell that Mamma was beginning to weaken and warm up to the idea of a shivaree and barn dance.

"The main thing is to keep it secret," said Trudy. "Right up to the last minute. I don't think we better even tell Karen. She might spill the beans."

"What did you say about me spilling beans," asked Karen, suddenly appearing in the kitchen doorway with a barnyard kitten in her arms.

They all laughed. Then Trudy pulled Karen over next to her chair, told her to bend down, and whispered something in her ear. "Now promise you won't tell Cora," she said.

"I won't," said Karen. "Who cares if you're embroidering dishtowels for Cora? That's probably what Tante Karen will give her too." Karen went back outside, no longer interested in the conversation, not looking behind to see Mamma and Marie concealing smiles.

"How come they decided to get married on the fourth of July anyway?" asked Trudy.

"That was Lars's idea," Marie said. "He's got a whole bunch of skyrockets and firecrackers and he told them since they couldn't afford to have a big wedding celebration, if they set their date for the fourth he'd fire everything off in honor of both their marriage and Independence Day. Milton liked the idea and that's when they set the date."

"Oh, boy, that's great," said Trudy. "Fireworks and a shivaree! Of course old Milton probably doesn't realize that the fourth of July will be the end of *his* independence."

They all laughed. Marie could see that Mamma was beginning to get into the spirit of the excitement of planning for a secret wedding celebration. *A shivaree!* Just the very name sent shivers of joy and anticipation through Marie. If it weren't for Trudy, nobody would have come up with anything that would be so much fun. Marie had never been to one, but she knew what a shivaree was like. People brought all kinds of household goods that they didn't want or need anymore. Sometimes couples got enough furniture, dishes, and stuff to furnish a house. People gave them new things, too, if they could afford to buy presents. You had to give Trudy credit. It was her idea. If Marie'd suggested it, she felt, Mamma would have dismissed the idea of a shivaree for Cora and Milton as something that they would think was too wild. Trudy sure knew how to talk to Mamma!

"We're going to need Lars and some other guys to help get the straw piled in one corner of the haymow so that we can have a barn dance," said Trudy. "We couldn't do it alone anyway because they'd know something was up. Can we trust Lars not to blab? Because we don't want Cora or Milton to ever suspect anything." Trudy looked a little worried.

"Lars will help and he'll keep quiet. So will Homer Merkel and Lyle Tornquist. They'll help Lars get the barn cleaned up and neither one of them will say anything about it to anybody. They don't blab, either one of them."

"Homer Merkel is sure cute, but if he's over here and I even say hello to him he gets red as a beet," said Trudy.

"Homer's bashful around girls he doesn't know," Marie explained, "especially if he kind of likes them."

95

"You think he likes me?" Trudy asked.

"I don't know," said Marie. "You never know about Homer."

It was Lyle Tornquist who really threw himself into the spirit of planning for the shivaree. He offered to do all the telephone calling from his house in town. Lyle knew a great deal about organizing a shivaree and what was needed to ensure its success. "We've got to have a kitchen kettle band with washboards and rain barrels to holler into too. I'll put a swell band together and I'll sing! I know just the song. Listen!" and Lyle began singing at the top of his lungs, since they were alone out in the barn, he and Marie and Trudy:

"Cora doesn't live here anymore!
    You must be the guy she waited for!
They told us we could tell you by the blue in your eye. . .
    checkered coat!
    flowered vest!
    striped pants!
    and polka dot tie!
You answer that description so I guess you're the guy . . .
But Cora doesn't live here anymore!"

"They sing that song to every guy who drives up to the barn and gets out of a car. The whole crowd sings it, and I don't think I ever went to a shivaree where that song was sung with whatever the bride's name was that the whole crowd didn't go crazy having fun," Lyle told them.

"Cora and Milton won't think that's a funny song to sing. They'll hate it. They'll just sit around acting lovey-dovey like they always do. *They* won't have any fun at a shivaree—anymore than they do any other place," said Marie.

"That's their tough luck," said Trudy, "but I bet you anything they'll enjoy it anyway. They'll get a lot of presents and that ought to make them happy. How you coming calling people, Lyle? Forget the preacher and his wife. Mrs. Carlsen plans to invite them for noon dinner and that's enough of having them around. They'd put a damper on the whole celebration according to Marie."

"That's right," said Marie. "Reverend Norgaard thinks anybody who dances will go straight to hell when they die."

"I wasn't going to ask them anyway," said Lyle. "How about Henry Byers? He lives across the road in our house now. Think we should ask him?"

"I guess we have to since we're asking Max and Myrtle. They'd think it was strange if we didn't invite Henry," said Marie.

"Okay, you can send him an invitation to the shivaree in the mail. I sure don't want to phone him and have to talk to him. Think he'll come? Think he'll get drunk and act nuts or something?"

"Not with Max around. He's afraid of Max and sometimes I think Myrtle won't put up with much with him either. Once I took the mail to their house and Henry was drunk and acting terrible. He was throwing dishes out of the cupboards and breaking them and Myrtle was screaming at him and telling him she was going to tell Max about him hiding booze in their house and. . . ."

"Okay, I don't want to hear about him, Marie," said Lyle. "Invite him if you want to but drunks can really spoil a shivaree. I've seen it happen. When things get rowdy, women want to go home and then all the fun's over. We don't want anyone at this shivaree who drinks too much and doesn't know how to behave."

"Henry will behave himself," promised Marie. "Max and Myrtle will make sure of that."

The Fourth of July shivaree and barn dance at the Carlsen farm was a huge success. Carloads of people with food, drink, and presents for the bride and groom kept coming with horns honking and whistles blowing. Marie had never heard such a din! People came in trucks and unloaded used furniture. Cora and Milton, stunned, stood together and smiled dazedly as they accepted congratulations and good wishes for a long and happy married life. The last guests did not leave until after three in the morning and Marie would remember Cora and Milton's wedding day as one of the most exciting events in her life. Thanks to Trudy, Cora and Milton's simple marriage plans had turned into rip-roaring celebration complete with Fourth of July fireworks. Who could ask for anything more? The only way it could have been better would have been if Rosie and Alfred had been home to join in the fun.

The next day, the fifth of July, Marie wrote and mailed long letters to Alfred and Rosie telling them all about Cora and Milton's exciting wedding including the fact that Henry Byers stayed sober. Alfred wrote back expressing pleasure in receiving Marie's letter giving all the details of the great news. Weeks went by but no answer came from Rosie.

❧ 12 ❧

Summer Dust 1934

"MARIE! TRUDY! GUESS WHAT!" AND WITHOUT GIVING THEM a chance to guess, Karen told them. "We got a letter in today's mail from both Rosie and Alfred. Rosie's not in Kansas anymore. She's in Chicago! Alfred's not driving a taxicab in California anymore. He's herding sheep in Montana. Mamma's still reading the letters!"

Karen burst into the bedroom on a hot day in late August. Marie and Trudy were propped up on Karen's double bed while they read movie magazines. Trudy had carried a big stack of scandal-filled periodicals dealing with the private lives of film stars out to the Carlsen farm. Trudy was an avid movie magazine reader. There was probably more known by Trudy Horton about the lives of Toby Wing, Joan Crawford, Clark Gable, and Errol Flynn than was known to the famous people themselves. Marie sometimes felt at a disadvantage when discussing the stars with Trudy because she did not have Trudy's extensive knowledge about the world of the rich and famous. Once Marie had said, "it says here that Joan Crawford never carries money in her purse because she's afraid she'll be tempted to buy candy! I never knew a movie star could be too poor to buy candy."

"Don't be silly, Marie," and Trudy had laughed. "She could buy a ton of candy and never miss the money. Joan Crawford doesn't want to eat candy because she doesn't want to get fat!"

Marie had felt silly for drawing the conclusion that Joan Crawford, like herself, passed up candy because of poverty. It was just that with the Depression, being poor seemed to be the reason why people couldn't buy things, even candy. Marie had to read piles of movie star magazines to keep up with Trudy on how people in Hollywood lived in their world of luxury and mysterious glamor. Marie felt only half the stories about movie stars were true. But down on the farm, movie magazines made interesting reading on the long, hot, dusty afternoons of summer.

Now that Karen had brought news that there were letters downstairs from Rosie and Alfred, Marie threw down her *Screen Stars* magazine. "Come on, Trudy," she cried. "Let's go down and read the letters from Rosie and Alfred. Who cares about what movie stars do anyway?"

Marie read Rosie's letter first. With much relief, she noticed that the envelope did have a return address up in the corner, Mrs. Rose Kravensky, c/o Mrs. Harold Hamilton, P. O. Box 1462, Evanston, Illinois. That was strange. Karen had said Rosie was in Chicago. But when she read the letter, Marie understood. Evanston was right next to Chicago and

Rosie was working as a waitress in Chicago. Marie read on. . . .

"Nick's aunt is living in a housekeeping room in Evanston and we're staying with her now. I don't know how long we'll stay with her because she doesn't have much room even for herself, but if you write in care of her she'll forward any letters you send on to me. She's pretty old but she's very nice and she loves Tommy. We can leave him with her when we're both working and that makes it nice. Nick has a temporary job as a part-time bellboy at a big Chicago hotel. It sure is hot here in Chicago, but it's a lot better than Kansas. You probably know about the dust bowl and how the wheat crops have been ruined. It was just so dry and hot and the dust got so bad, we decided to leave and Nick thought Chicago with his aunt might be a good place, but maybe we can come to Iowa before Christmas. . . ."

Marie stopped reading Rosie's letter and turned to Mamma, "Why does Nick always decide where they should go? Why couldn't Rosie tell him she wanted to come home instead of going to live with his aunt in Chicago?"

"She is married, Marie," said Mamma. "She must go with her husband. It is the man who must find the kind of work that will support his family. Women have never earned much money no matter what job they do. Women have always had to follow their husbands, Marie. Let us hope Nick can find a better job."

"Well, I won't," said Marie. "When I grow up I'm going to decide where I want to live and I'm not going to move every time some man tells me I have to go live with his aunt or somebody."

"Then you better have a job that pays a lot of money,"

said Trudy. "I'm going to keep my eye out for a rich husband."

"Well, you won't find one around here," said Marie. "Rosie could have married Henry Byers, but you wouldn't want him, Trudy. He's rich but he's a jerk."

Marie finished reading Rosie's letter. She'd received Marie's letter about Cora's wedding and was really tickled about the shivaree. How she wished she could have been home on the Fourth of July. Well, maybe Thanksgiving or Christmas, Rosie hoped. Everybody keep your fingers crossed, maybe she'd be home by then, and Rosie had signed her letter . . . "Love all of you forever, Rosie."

Alfred's letter was more cheerful. He liked Montana. There were no electrician jobs on the big government dam that was being built, but he had found a job as a sort of combination bookkeeper and sheepherder on a big Montana ranch . . . not at all like the Middle West farms. The big open spaces of Montana were beautiful beyond description according to Alfred. It was so quiet and restful to be living in there. Yes, Alfred was happy seeing for himself the great many different ways that people lived in the United States. A real education, Alfred said, and one you could never get from reading books.

Marie spent the rest of that long hot dusty August afternoon writing letters to both Rosie and Alfred. She wrote such long letters that she supposed she'd have to have the letters weighed in the Spencer post office. She wouldn't be a bit surprised if each letter would need *two* three-cent stamps. It gave her a great deal of satisfaction when she went to the post office in town and found out she was right. She had to spend twelve cents for postage. It was worth it! She thought both Alfred and Rosie would write back to her right away after receiving such volumes of news from home.

Marie was right about Alfred . . . wrong about Rosie. By the time school started in September, she had received a long letter and a postcard showing grazing sheep from Alfred. By the end of September, not one letter or even a one-cent postcard came from Rosie. Marie had eagerly checked for a letter each weekday during the month of September and into October. She never asked Mamma or anybody else why doesn't Rosie write? Nobody would have the answer to that question so there was no use asking it. Marie just kept opening the mailbox and kept hoping for mail from Rosie.

ᘿ 13 ᘾ

The Box Social

THE BOX SOCIAL WAS SCHEDULED TO BE HELD AT RIVERTON township school district number Five right before Halloween. Money was badly needed to buy school supplies such as new maps, books, another coal bucket, and more rural school necessities than the Clay County school budget could provide. The upper grade students were assigned the task of designing and printing the invitations.

Since Marie was now in eighth grade and artistic, according to Miss Eriksen, the major responsibility of making box social invitations fell to her. Fifty invitations were sent to friends of Cloverdale School, District #5, to people who lived in Riverton Township and in the city of Spencer. Some invitations were hand delivered by students and others were sent in the mail.

"Shall we send one to the Clarke family?" asked Marie.

"They live across the field from us now but they don't know many neighbors. They're really nice!"

"By all means. Invite them," said Miss Eriksen. "This will be a wonderful way for them to get better acquainted."

Marie took special care with the Clarke invitation. She designed a beautiful box social message showing a colorfully decorated box and urging attendance with "Join the Fun" printed in varied colors. No doubt about it, the Clarke invitation was her masterpiece of art for the day. How Marie hoped Bobby Clarke would come, make the highest bid for her box, and then she and Bobby would sit together and eat the contents.

Cora had all kinds of colored crepe paper, white tissue paper, ribbons, and boxes upstairs in a closet, which she had not yet moved to her house in Everly. She used these things for holiday decorations at her own school in Summit Township.

How could she make sure that Bobby Clarke would bid on her box? The box social auctioneer would call out a number that was on the box and the girl or woman with that number would come forward after somebody bid the highest for the box, and then they'd sit together and eat whatever was in it. Mamma was going to put fried chicken, potato salad, homemade bread, and chocolate cake in all the Carlsen boxes.

Marie put white tissue paper all around her box, gluing it neatly and securely; then she fashioned pink roses out of the crepe paper, green leaves from construction paper, and glued roses and leaves on the sides and top of the box. She selected a green satin ribbon to tie around the box after it was filled with the best food anybody could make. Nobody could make chocolate cake with fudge icing or fry chicken as golden brown and crisp any better than Mamma. Then Marie had a great idea! She'd tell Lyle to tell Bobby Clarke that the best food would be in the box decorated with lots of pink roses on white tissue paper and tied with a green satin bow. Marie knew one thing about men and boys! Most of them (and Bobby Clarke was probably no different) wouldn't care two hoots which woman or girl they ate supper with. They were mainly interested in something good to eat and they always figured that the boxes that were decorated the best contained the most appetizing box-social food.

Cora didn't plan to go to the box social. Marie generously offered to decorate boxes for Mamma, Karen, and also one for Trudy whom Karen had invited to go with them. Of course, Marie felt there was no need to work so hard on the other three boxes. She'd just make a single rose (one red, one yellow, one white) to decorate those. When she was finished, she was quite sure that the best-decorated box at the social would be the one she hoped to share with Bobby Clarke.

All the boxes were delivered (wrapped or in brown paper sacks) to Miss Eriksen. She numbered them and gave the corresponding number to the woman or girl providing the box—Marie's number was twelve. Lyle laughed when she told him to tell Bobby Clarke to bid on number twelve because it would have the best food.

"Okay, I know you're worried that you might have to eat with Henry Byers. I'll tell about four other guys to bid on number twelve too. But I'm going to bid on Ma's box. She put banana cream pie in her's and she wouldn't let us cut into it before we left tonight."

The Box Social

There was a big crowd in the schoolhouse, far too many for the number of desks in the one-room school. Most of the people were either standing or sitting on the floor. Marie saw Bobby Clarke standing in the back of the room beside a very pretty blond girl. Marie wondered who she was.

Max Byers was the auctioneer. He had a loud voice and a way of urging the bidding to the highest possible price. "Now remember, this box social is for a good cause. All the proceeds go to buy supplies and equipment for the school. The kids deserve the best! What am I bid for this beautiful green box with the orange yarn bow. This is a very heavy box. I'll bet there's a whole roasted chicken in here. Who'll start the bidding at one dollar. Do I hear one dollar?"

"One dollar," yelled a man Marie didn't know.

"One dollar and a quarter," called out Henry Byers.

The box went to the first bidder at two dollars after the bid went up a dime or a nickel at a time. The box had been provided by Dorothy Rose Knight and she made a face as she went up to claim her box and eating partner, a tall hungry-looking farmhand who worked for Max Byers.

Marie was standing by Trudy along the wall. She noted with satisfaction that Bobby Clarke had not yet made a bid on any of the boxes that Max Byers had put up for auction. That probably meant that Lyle had told him which one to bid for and he was waiting for the one with all the pink roses. Marie's box!

Then Max picked Marie's beautifully decorated box off the table. "The prettiest box yet!" he called. "Bet it's full of mouth-watering home cooking and baking! Who'll start the bidding at a dollar? Do I hear one dollar?"

107

One bid after another was called until the bidding reached three dollars. But Bobby Clarke did not bid on Marie's box. Not once did he open his mouth or raise his hand to indicate that he was in the bidding for the pink rose-covered box.

"Three dollars and ten cents," called a voice Marie identified as Red Gillette's. There was silence now and Marie's heart seemed to stand still. If not Bobby Clarke, she hoped the high bidder for her box would be Red Gillette.

"Sold!" yelled Max Byers. "Sold to Red Gillette for three dollars and ten cents!"

Marie stepped forward. "Oh," moaned Red Gillette. "I never knew it was her's. I thought it was Angeline's."

Never in her life had Marie felt such humiliation and some people who heard what Red Gillette said laughed. Even Max Byers laughed. "Well, now, we can't all eat with Angeline even though she might be our choice as the beauty among beauties," Max said.

Almost every man and boy who didn't already have a partner bid on the pale blue box decorated with gold stars and a gold ribbon. Bobby Clarke kept bidding it up to eight dollars. Of course it was Angeline Carter's box, the beautiful girl standing beside Bobby Clarke. Then Max Byers made a bid himself of fifteen dollars. The bidding stopped. Every man and boy knew that nobody was going higher than Max, the richest person in the room. Angeline came tripping forward and gave Max a little peck of a kiss on his cheek.

"Don't that make you sick," whispered Trudy to Marie. "She acts like she thinks she's Jean Harlow or somebody!"

Max went on auctioning off boxes, but after Angeline's,

no box went any higher than three dollars. None were as beautifully decorated either, except perhaps Marie's and now she wasn't at all sure of that. Trudy's box with the red rose went for $2.50 to Henry Byers. Mr. Knight bid the highest for Mamma's box and Karen's box went to Johnny Merkel, Homer's father. Everyone was apparently happy with whoever was to be a supper partner except Red Gillette.

"I hope you've got something worth eating in that box." Red Gillette said to Marie within Max Byers's hearing.

"There's chicken and chocolate cake," said Marie, "and you can have all of it, because I'm not going to eat with you!"

If he was disappointed because he hadn't gotten to eat with beautiful Angeline Carter, Marie certainly wasn't going to act thrilled to be his box-social partner. Next to Bobby Clarke, Red Gillette was no big deal and she might as well let him know it. Suddenly, Max Byers thought he'd come up with a great idea to make more money for the box-social fund raiser.

"All right then. Listen everyone . . . as the auctioneer, I donate this beautiful box that I paid fifteen dollars for and whoever bids the highest this time will get the box and the pleasure of Miss Angeline Carter's company. Those of you who did not purchase a box may help yourself to sandwiches and coffee or milk at the buffet table provided by the ladies of the school district."

The bid on Angeline Carter's box reached six dollars this time and the lucky winner was Bobby Clarke. The highest Red Gillette would go was two dollars since he'd already spent three dollars and ten cents on Marie's box.

"Too bad," laughed Trudy. "He sure wanted to eat with old Angeline. She's at least twenty-five. Anyway, I heard she's Bobby Clarke's steady girlfriend so what did Red Gillette expect?"

Red Gillette wasted no time in tearing apart Marie's work of art, the box-social box she'd spent so much time decorating, and began eating a chicken breast. He handed Marie a drumstick. "Here," he said, "you might as well have something to eat. I don't need to eat it all."

"All right," said Marie because she was hungry. Red Gillette was cute, but when it came to manners he sure had a lot to learn! And what was worse, he didn't even know that he didn't know how to treat a girl.

Marie had one consolation. At least she didn't have to share her box with fat, repulsive Henry Byers. That would have been worse. Now she looked over at Trudy and Henry, sitting together on a couple of folding chairs Henry had found for them, and to her surprise they seemed to be enjoying themselves as they ate the contents of Trudy's box. Of course, thought Marie, Henry and Trudy would be happy with anybody as long as they were eating good food.

At the end of the box social evening, Henry offered to drive Trudy home and she accepted. Marie rode home with Lars, Mamma, and Karen. It wasn't yet ten o'clock but Marie went directly up to bed. She didn't cry. She thought about how both Bobby Clarke and Red Gillette were so attracted to Angeline Carter who did look a little like Jean Harlow. Who cares? Neither one of them could hold a candle to Ken Maynard, the cowboy movie star of her dreams. Marie went to sleep thinking how wonderful it would be to be riding behind him on his white horse as they galloped into the sunset after capturing the rustlers who by some strange coincidence had faces like Red Gillette, Bobby Clarke, and Henry Byers.

14

Myrtle's Influence

FOR THE SCHOOL DISTRICT, THE BOX SOCIAL WAS A GREAT
financial success. Enough money had been raised to buy much-
needed supplies, a used set of encyclopedias, and many new
books, fiction, poetry, and nonfiction, for the school library.
As far as Marie was concerned, she was a little soured on
considering romantic involvement with either Bobby Clarke
or Red Gillette. After all, neither of them were anything but
farm boys!

Sir Walter Scott's novels were among the books Miss
Eriksen purchased with the box-social money. Bobby Clarke
and Red Gillette, Marie realized, had absolutely nothing in
common with the legendary knights—Ivanhoe, for example—
who accomplished great deeds. Even Ken Maynard paled in
comparison with the chivalry of the Scottish knights in *The
Lady of The Lake*.

The box social also brought into public notice the romance between Myrtle Byers and Johnny Merkel. Although Johnny Merkel had bid the highest on Karen's box and had eaten with her, he had been observed later holding hands with Myrtle Byers. Since Myrtle, to anyone's knowledge had never before had a boyfriend, she was considered an old maid. Naturally, speculation on possible matrimony for Myrtle and Johnny became a common topic of neighborhood conversation. Several things contributed to gossip that the couple were considering marriage.

Johnny's wife had died more than two years ago. All of his seven children, except Homer, who still lived with Johnny, had been divided up among Mrs. Merkel's mother and sisters who lived in Greenville. Myrtle had been very kind to Johnny and Homer and had washed and ironed, cooked and baked, and cleaned the Merkel house in the name of charity. Now it appeared to be in the name of love!

"Myrtle's crazy about Johnny Merkel," said Karen. "She'd give anything to marry him!"

"Who says?" asked Marie.

"Dorothy Rose Knight! She said her mother said so."

"Her mother is always talking about somebody. You can't believe anything Dorothy Rose says that she got from her mother."

Yet there were other indications of Myrtle's interest in the Merkel family that Marie took more seriously. Myrtle had convinced Homer Merkel that he had to go to high school and Homer now walked up the dirt road from his house to the schoolhouse corner, met the Knight boys in their 1926 Hupmobile, and rode with the Knights and Lars into Spencer to high school. Myrtle also gave Homer piano lessons at her house. Free! Another thing, Homer had changed his opinion of Myrtle Byers. His manners were better than any other farm boy Marie knew. He had even told Mrs. Carlsen that Myrtle Byers was "a very nice lady."

Homer Merkel was still one of Lars's best friends and he often stopped off with Lars at the Carlsen driveway when the Knight boys drove them home from high school. Then Homer would visit with Lars, Mamma, Marie, and Karen, or whoever was home before he cut across the fields to do chores at his own home along the dirt road. From Homer Marie learned some very interesting news.

"Myrtle's going with me and Pa over to Grandma Flack's in Greenville for Thanksgiving. The whole family is going to be there so we can all be together. Millie and Darlene like living with my aunt and uncle and they're going to stay with them. Arlo's got a lot of friends and likes going to school where he is with my other aunt and uncle so he'll keep on living with them. But me and Pa and Myrtle are going to bring the little kids who don't go to school yet, Jimmy Lee and Bonnie, home with us after Thanksgiving. Myrtle's going to take care of them at her house."

"How about Frannie?" asked Marie.

"Frannie wants to keep on living with Grandma Flack. They get along fine. Grandma Flack teaches Frannie to do a lot of things that she never could learn before. But Grandma says she's just getting too old to take care of the little kids, that they make so much work and she gets tired. She told Pa she didn't know what to do about them and when Pa told Myrtle, she said she'd be glad to take care of them until he got a housekeeper but Pa don't know when he can afford to do that so Myrtle will probably keep them for quite awhile."

"Myrtle likes babies a lot," said Marie. "She'll take real good care of them because Myrtle likes to do things for people."

"I know," said Homer. "Myrtle's a good lady."

After Thanksgiving, Marie went over to the Byers's big house along the gravel road to see Myrtle and Jimmy Lee and Bonnie Merkel. Jimmy Lee was three now and Bonnie was five. It seemed kind of strange to Marie. It was as if the littlest Merkel kids belonged to Myrtle Byers now. She'd bought them cute clothes, fixed up the upstairs bedroom that used to be Henry's before he moved into the Tornquist house, and made the room into a nursery playroom with all kinds of toys. Anybody could tell that Myrtle Byers was really happy taking care of the little Merkels.

"Aren't they sweet?" said Myrtle Byers, "and they're just as good as gold. Poor little lambs were just starved for love."

The only person who was really upset about Myrtle taking care of the little Merkel kids was Henry Byers. Marie learned about that from Trudy Horton who, ever since the box social, had been going to the movies with Henry on Saturday nights.

"Why do you go with him?" Marie had asked. "He's a big fat jerk, selfish and mean. I should know. My sister Rosie was engaged to him once."

"Nobody's perfect," laughed Trudy, "but I know what you mean. Henry's madder than hops about Myrtle putting the Merkel kids in his old bedroom and fixing it up like a nursery."

"Why should he care?" Marie asked. "He doesn't live there anymore. He lives across the highway in the Tornquists' house."

"Henry says someday he'll inherit that house from his father and he doesn't want his home turned into an orphanage. He even went out and had a big fight with Myrtle about it and she told him to go peddle his papers. That's exactly what she said 'go peddle your papers, Henry' and that really burned him up. Henry says Myrtle has too much influence over his father and he thinks she's turning him against him."

"Henry turns everybody against him all by himself," said Marie, "and if I were you, Trudy, I wouldn't go to the show or anyplace with that fat jerk."

"I'm sixteen now," said Trudy. "I can't get into the movies at kid prices anymore and I don't have seventy-five cents or a dollar to go on Saturday night. I don't even have fifty or sixty cents to go in the afternoon even before the price goes up. Henry pays my way. That's why I go with him! He pays my way. Anyway, compared to old Jake, Henry's not so bad."

Marie thought Trudy had changed since her sixteenth birthday in September. She wore a lot of lipstick and rouge, wore tighter sweaters and skirts, and she smoked! Not around anybody except Marie and she made her promise not to tell. Trudy smoked Camels, Henry's brand, and she admitted to Marie that Henry supplied her with cigarettes. Now that Trudy had started dating Henry Byers, she spent less time at the Carlsen farm. Marie decided she didn't care. She had other friends!

Yet Marie missed Trudy that fall. Of course, the person Marie missed the most was Rosie. She kept opening the mailbox, hoping for a letter. When none came, she continued to hope and pray that Rosie and Nick and the baby would come home some day very soon or at least before Christmas.

116

◈ 15 ◈

Christmas 1934 and Surprises

ONE COLD WINTER DAY WITH CHRISTMAS DRAWING NEAR, Marie came home from school, shook the snow from her overshoes before she entered the house, and looked with surprise at a suitcase by the telephone stand. She recognized it immediately. Alfred was home! It was a great surprise to everyone. He hadn't written that he was coming.

He looked different. Bigger somehow. And much older even though he had only been gone two years. He had left just before Christmas in 1932 and now he was back, just before Christmas in 1934. He almost seemed like a stranger. Very polite to Mamma, sitting at the kitchen table, drinking his coffee black because that was the way he liked it now.

"I've done a little wiring here and there and could always pick up some extra money fixing radios that needed repairing. I know the trade and can always fall back on that line of work. But right now I want to get back to farming. This is where I belong. As far as I'm concerned, Ma, this is the best state in the union. We've got everything here we need. I guess a guy has to go away before he realizes that the grass isn't greener on the other side of the fence."

Alfred had come home to stay. Since corn picking, when Hans moved on to help Uncle Soren, Lars had been doing the chores before and after school without the help of a hired man. That meant there was nobody using Alfred's room and after supper, Alfred carried his suitcase upstairs and unpacked his clothes. Marie and Karen sat on the big cretonne-covered trunk that always held the winter quilts and blankets and watched their older brother take things out of his suitcase and hang shirts and suits in his closet.

"Oh, here's something I bought for you, Marie," he said, handing her a long, flat, narrow box.

"P A S T E L S" it said on the cover. It was a box of colored chalk; soft chalk in every color and hue in the rainbow. Marie was delighted that Alfred had remembered that she wanted to become an artist.

"Thanks, Alfred," she said. "I never knew there was anything like this. Better than crayons, so many more shades of colors. I really like them!"

"I thought you would," said Alfred. "When we go into town, I'll get you some big sheets of white paper to draw on. Out West I knew a guy who made pictures with chalk like this. They turned out real pretty and he'd sell them for a dollar each. He was just a sheepherder like me, and he said it made a nice hobby, making scenes from nature. I know how lonesome a guy can get out there by himself if he doesn't have something to entertain himself. I never had any artistic talent but I used to read a lot to pass the time."

Alfred gave Karen a cowgirl doll and she was pleased. Alfred liked to give presents and he had something in his suitcase for everybody in the family. "Figure you might as well have your Christmas presents early," he laughed. "It'll save me the price of wrapping paper."

It was good to have Alfred home again. But it was different. Marie felt almost shy around him. Now that she was in eighth grade, she didn't need him the way she did when she was much younger, before he went away. Whether Alfred noticed or not, Marie realized she didn't need to hang around him anymore, didn't need him to fight her battles for her. She was no longer a little kid who needed an older brother to take her places. Of course, if Alfred wanted to buy her some paper to draw on, it was okay. She was eager to try making some landscape scenes with the pastels and if they turned out well, she'd give one to Miss Eriksen for a Christmas present. Her teacher was the one who always told her maybe someday she'd be an artist. Marie thought of all the beautiful sunsets she'd seen from the pighouse roof and wouldn't it be fun to make that kind of picture with the wide range of colors in the box of pastels?

Cora and Milton came from Everly with Christmas-paper wrapped packages for everyone and put them under the big Christmas tree that Lars and Alfred had found somewhere and chopped down and hauled home. Marie and Karen had strung popcorn and made red and green construction paper decorations to hang on it. When they put on the electric lights and the star on the top, Marie thought it was the prettiest tree they'd ever had. There was roast goose and mincemeat pie and the relatives—Uncle Soren and Uncle Chris and Tante Karen, whose disposition always improved during the holidays—came for supper to make the Christmas season joyful.

There was only one reason to feel sad. There was not even a Christmas card from Rosie. Christmas passed without word from her. It seemed better not to talk about her. Not to worry too much. It was better, Marie decided, to hope that without any expectation of when, suddenly Rosie would appear in the dining room or kitchen when she came home from school some night. Just like Alfred, Marie thought, she might come home someday and surprise everybody! And when she did, Nick and the baby would probably be with her.

January and February of 1935 passed slowly much as they had in other years for Marie. The only difference, it seemed, as she walked along Highway 71 to and from the country schoolhouse, was that the snowdrifts were piled much higher, it was even more bitter cold, and the wind against her face was much sharper. Marie had one consolation, and one only, that this was positively the last cold winter she would have to walk along this Iowa highway to a rural school. Just a few months away in the spring, in May, she would graduate from eighth grade and in the fall she would ride to school in a car. She would be a high school student like Lars, Norman and Lyle Tornquist, and Red Gillette. She thought about how Red had treated her at the box social but remembered without malice. He probably couldn't help it. Farm boys were not known for good manners and Angeline Carter did look like Jean Harlowe! Angeline and Bobby Clarke were engaged to be married in June. That left Red Gillette to Marie. Maybe . . . when he saw her in high school he'd decide he liked her again!

A big surprise came in March. There was a very thick letter in the mailbox from Rosie! Nick, Rosie, and Nick's aunt had been moving around all winter, harvesting fruits and vegetables, in Florida and Texas, wherever they could find work. Rosie didn't mention a word about why she hadn't written or even sent a card at Christmas. She just wrote about all the places they'd worked and the things they'd seen.

There had been one encouraging thing about the letter and Marie read that part of the letter over and over. "We're heading north now and we'll be coming home this summer for sure. Nick promised I could go home when we go back to Illinois. It won't be long now and I'll be back with all of you. I miss everybody so much!"

Marie wrote a long letter to Rosie. She sent snapshots that Cora had taken of the family with her Brownie camera. It didn't matter so much now if Rosie didn't get around to answering her letter. She would be home this summer! That was the important thing. Rosie was coming home and Rosie kept her promises! Marie addressed her letter to Mrs. Rose Kravensky (in care of a Mr. Andrew Parks) to a post office box in Fort Worth, Texas, which Rosie had written as a return address. They might not stay in Texas much longer, but she hoped somebody would write to her Rosie had said. Marie was relieved and happy when she put a stamp on the envelope and mailed her letter to Rosie. "Can hardly wait for summer, Love, Marie," she'd signed it.

❧ 16 ❧

On the Way to Being Grown Up

MAY CAME WITH ALL THE SUNNY FRESHNESS OF AN IOWA spring. The rainstorms of April were over. May had always been Marie's favorite month because it meant her birthday, and the end of May brought summer vacation from school. This May was really special because the first Sunday in May would be when her Sunday school class would be confirmed. Then, Marie would celebrate her fourteenth birthday on the eighth of May. Finally, the last week in May, on the day of the Riverton Township picnic, she would, at long last, graduate from eighth grade and be ready to start high school in town in the fall.

It seemed to Marie that this May was the one she'd been waiting for all her life. She would finally be done with country school and well on her way to being grown up like her older sisters, Cora and Rosie. Marie felt very happy. Nothing could dampen her spirits now. The letter she'd been waiting for was in the mailbox! The big pink envelope, with Rosie's familiar handwriting, was folded inside the Des Moines Register newspaper. It was a birthday card. Marie was sure of that!

If the letter contained the news Marie hoped for, she'd be the happiest kid in Iowa, in the United States of America, and maybe in the whole world! It was noon and Marie was alone at the mailbox. Karen was in fifth grade now and she always took her lunch to school so that she could hang around with her best friend. Marie really didn't have a special friend in school, boy or girl. Marie realized now, as she fought the temptation to tear the envelope open and read her sister's letter quickly, that Rosie was the best friend she'd ever had in her life. How she hoped the letter would say that Rosie, Nick, and the baby were planning to come home!

She could wait! When she got home for noon lunch, she'd read the letter. It was nice to prolong the wonderful feeling of anticipation of reading Rosie's letter with its promise to come home this summer and maybe telling now exactly when the family could expect to see her and the baby.

When Marie reached the Tornquist farm driveway, the collie dog, Joe, ran out to meet her. Joe was wagging his tail and Marie petted his head. Now that Lyle was a freshman in high school and lived in town, Marie didn't see him very much. She missed him. She knew his collie dog missed him, too, and that Joe knew she was Lyle's friend. Joe had refused to move to town and was always running away back to his farm home so Henry Byers had consented to keep him as a watchdog. Marie hoped Henry was good to Joe because the Tornquists had had him for more than eight years and he was the brother of the Carlsen's dog, Jimmy. Maybe that was why Joe wouldn't move to town. Maybe he didn't want to leave Jimmy.

Marie never brought Henry Byers's mail to him. She'd never liked him. Let the fat slob get his own mail, she always thought when she walked past the house he now lived in and she wished that the Tornquists had not moved. Marie ran up the long evergreen-lined driveway of her own home, past the house, down through the grove of trees, and climbed up on the pighouse roof. She didn't want to share her birthday card and letter from Rosie with anybody until she had a chance to spend all the time she wanted reading it herself. The card was beautiful and signed "Love, Rosie, Nick, and Tommy." The letter was short but the news was wonderful. They were coming home for sure in August! Marie ran quickly to the house and gave Mamma the card and letter. Mamma put on her reading glasses and read the letter from Rosie over and over. "So she is finally coming home and I will get to see my grandchild. That is good news!" Marie knew Mamma was just as happy and excited as she was.

Marie wore a new white dress with a satin collar the Sunday of her confirmation. The surprising thing was how kindly Reverend Norgaard treated the whole class after they were confirmed. He had a party for them at his house with cake and ice cream and he treated all of them in a very friendly and pleasant manner. "I know I have been hard on you," he said when he cut the cake, "but you have been one of my best confirmation classes. You have all memorized your catechism lessons well and even though you cannot possibly, at your age, understand all that it means, you will know and remember the words as I have taught you. When you are much older you will have the knowledge to understand what you have learned and it will preserve your faith in God Almighty." He even wrote in her new Bible, a present from the Ladies Aid Society and the preacher, "For my dear friend, Marie Carlsen, from Reverend Kai Norgaard and the Bethany Lutheran Ladies Aid." Well, she supposed she could be his friend now that she no longer had to go to him for confirmation class. Now they were adult members of the church! Marie could start thinking about graduation from eighth grade.

Marie loved poems by Longfellow. She chose his poem "The Builders" to recite at her eighth grade graduation. She went to the pighouse roof where she could be alone and project her voice, loud and with conviction, across the broad expanse of the pigyard, startling the wits out of the pigs, her captive audience, while she memorized her oration. Marie recited . . . "I have chosen to give as my oration a poem by Henry Wadsworth Longfellow:

> 'The Builders
>
> All are architects of Fate
> Working in these Walls of Time
> Some with massive deeds and great,
> Some with ornaments of rhyme.
> Nothing useless is, or low . . .' "

The pigs became accustomed to hearing the stirring oration after awhile. She'd practiced the poem over and over again.

They just grunted, waddled around, and used their snouts to dig holes in the mud. Marie decided that pigs *were* too useless and low to appreciate Longfellow, but it would be different when she recited the poem before a real audience at her eighth grade graduation. She would say it perfectly and with expression! Marie imagined the audience clapping long after she sat down. It was quite possible that her oration would be the best one!

A letter came from Rosie toward the end of May. It was full of news about all the different jobs she and Nick had done, moving from place to place as field workers and even working for a carnival. Now they were working near Chicago. The return address was a post office box in a town in Illinois. Marie wrote Rosie a long letter, happy that when Rosie, Nick, and the baby came home in August, she'd be ready for high school. Eighth grade graduation would be over.

It was over. The township picnic and her eighth grade graduation were now memories. It should have been the best performance of her life but it was definitely the worst! Marie sat on the pighouse roof and she felt miserable. *Life for her was hopeless!*

She'd never be anything! Marie realized that now. She sat on the pighouse roof and gazed over the far expanse of cornfields stretching on forever and ever.

What had ever made her think she could be somebody? Get off the farm? Leave? Go to New York City or out West to California. Now she knew it had all been a foolish dream!

All are architects of Fate
   Working in these Walls of Time
Some with massive deeds and great,
   Some with ornaments of rhyme.

Nothing useless is, or low,
   Each thing in its place is best
And what seems but idle show
   Strengthens and supports the rest.
For the structure that we raise. . . .

Then no more words came. She hadn't been able to remember. She couldn't think! The humiliation! The horrible realization of failure! Waiting . . . the silence . . . no words would come. She couldn't remember! She, Marie, who could remember everybody's part in every Sunday school play since she was six, forgot her graduation oration! Right in the middle she'd forgotten which line came next. She'd forgotten almost the whole poem. She'd said it perfectly a hundred times to herself on the pighouse roof; but there on the stage, standing alone in front of more than a hundred people, she couldn't remember the next line. She forgot everything she ever knew!

She'd looked out at hundreds of heads with all the eyes looking at her, with every ear waiting for the sound of her voice to continue, and nothing happened. . . . Nobody laughed! Nobody talked! Nobody coughed! They just waited while she stood, the only one standing, and they waited for her to remember. There was nobody to help her, no teacher or other kid from school to prompt her with a loud whisper, not up on the graduation stage. Finally, after what seemed forever, she remembered the end, the last few lines. . . .

> Thus alone can we attain
>   To those turrets, where the eye
> Sees the world as one vast plain,
>   And one boundless reach of sky.

They applauded. The whole audience clapped politely when she sat down. She felt nothing but humiliation and shame as she returned to the folding chair. There she sat, with about fifteen other eighth grade graduates and listened to them while they spoke their orations one by one. Every one remembered perfectly. Marie had been the only one who forgot. And they knew! The whole audience, everybody at the township eighth grade graduation knew it was wrong! But they'd clapped anyway, because they'd felt sorry for her. They'd pitied her because she was too stupid to remember.

She'd forgotten because she was first. If only she hadn't been introduced as the graduate with the highest grades and called to go first. That must have been what frightened her so much, being the one to go first.

Now, still wearing the light blue graduation dress with the pink rose pinned on it, Marie sat on the pighouse roof and looked at the vast plain of Iowa and beyond to the "boundless reach of sky." She'd come here and climbed up on the roof as soon as she'd come home from the township picnic and her eighth grade graduation because she had to be alone. Her humiliation had been too great to be reminded of it by anybody in the family. She wondered forlornly if she would go on feeling as miserable as she did today for the rest of her life. Graduation was supposed to be so wonderful and it had been so terrible.

Finally Marie climbed down from the pighouse roof, not caring what happened to her blue crepe dress, which she'd loved . . . not even if she tore it on a nail. Lars was the only one in the kitchen. He was eating a bowl of cornflakes before supper.

"Karen said you stood on the stage and forgot the whole poem."

"Shut up!" Marie yelled and ran upstairs to change her dress.

Lars laughed and Marie was too mad to cry.

Strangely enough it was Trudy Horton, in her frank and earnest way, who put the matter of Marie's eighth grade graduation in proper perspective. Lars enjoyed reconstructing what happened for anyone who might have missed the program.

"Did you hear how Marie made a fool of herself up on the stage, Trudy, with the whole township watching?"

"What'd she do?" asked Trudy.

"She forgot practically the whole poem."

"Shoot!" said Trudy in exasperation. "You think that's bad? That's nothing! So who even notices or cares two hoots about a thing like that? Let me tell you what happened in the church at Royal when I was confirmed. A girl started having her period, that's what! Blood all over the back of her white dress when she went to the rail to kneel for communion. The whole church saw the blood and the preacher was saying, "this is My Body—this is My Blood!"

"Leave it to Trudy," laughed Cora when Marie told her what Trudy had said—and that it had the effect of shutting Lars up about the subject of Marie's graduation. "Things can always be worse."

"I guess so," said Marie, remembering how Trudy had continued, reminding Lars that forgetting a poem was not as stupid as having to take eighth grade over "like some people I know" and Lars suddenly remembered that he had chores to do outside the house. Marie was glad she'd told Trudy that Lars had flunked eighth grade. He never mentioned Marie's graduation again.

🐦 17 🐦

Henry's Choice

AFTER ALL THE SPECIAL EVENTS OF MAY—HER BIRTHDAY, then confirmation, and finally the big day of her graduation from eighth grade—June seemed extremely boring to Marie. She'd worked in the garden, pulling weeds and picking strawberries. She'd helped Mamma clean, paint, and varnish in the house, and she'd even helped Cora clean her house in Everly after school was out.

Fourth of July this year, 1935, unlike the fun of Cora and Milton's shivaree wedding celebration on last year's Fourth of July, was hardly worth writing to Rosie about. The whole family, Mamma, Alfred, Karen, Lars, Marie, and even Cora and Milton had spent the Fourth of July at Tante Karen's summer cottage at Lake Okoboji. Uncle Chris was there and so was Hans Petersen, the hired man from Denmark, as well as Uncle Soren. Marie went to the amusement park with

Karen and rode on the Ferris wheel and the roller coaster. They went swimming, and remembering the time last year with Trudy when she'd almost drowned, Marie had a fear of water and stayed near the beach. She envied the good swimmers, including Karen, who splashed and squealed as they climbed up on the raft and dived into deep water. Marie sat alone on the beach and realized that there was nothing so great about being fourteen when you no longer enjoyed even going to the lake. Life was such a bore!

Now that Trudy had a cooking job at the hotel she no longer came out to the farm so often. Lyle Tornquist lived in town now and Red Gillette probably went to see him at his house in Spencer. Anyway, he never bothered to come to the Carlsen farm to see Marie. Why should he? He'd probably heard about how stupid she was, forgetting the poem. Not only was she skinny and plain, Marie thought, but she was probably not nearly as smart as the kids who lived in town and went to school there.

She thought about Trudy. She'd never gone to high school but she was smart when it came to telling people what she thought. Marie wished she had Trudy's nerve. Trudy'd been smart enough to stop going with Henry Byers when she found out for herself what he was really like. Now she had a lot of other boyfriends, some with cars who took her to the movies and dances. Homer Merkel had gotten over his bashfulness enough to ask Trudy for a date. Trudy said she really liked Homer, that they always had fun together. *Good for them,* Marie thought. She supposed she should be glad some people were enjoying the summer. She sure wasn't!

July dragged by, dry and hot, that summer of 1935. There was never a letter in the mail from Rosie. How long had it been since she'd written? Not since the end of May. When she'd promised again that she'd be coming home this summer, Marie had written to Rosie then and the letter hadn't come back marked "moved—address unknown" or anything. Marie wondered if Rosie had ever received the letter she'd written to her in May. She really didn't blame Rosie for not writing more often. Marie realized that working in the fields, moving around so much, time was probably going by so fast for Rosie that she didn't realize how long it had been since she'd written home. She'd write when she got around to doing it. She'd come home too . . . some day. Maybe when hard times were over and Nick could settle himself.

One Saturday about the middle of July, Lars was talking to Mamma in the kitchen. He said he and Homer Merkel had seen Max Byers uptown and he wanted them to do some work for him.

"Max said he'd give me and Homer each a dollar if we'd clean out his barn this afternoon. Is that okay, Ma?"

"All right, Lars," said Mamma. "It is too bad that a man like Max should have such a useless son as Henry. Max helps him so much but he does nothing for his father. You help Max but tell him he does not have to pay you."

"Sure, I can tell him but Max never lets anybody work for him without paying them," Lars said and smiled.

"Can I go over and help Lars and Homer?" asked Marie. She needed to go somewhere. She was so bored. Besides it had been a long time since she'd seen Myrtle and the little Merkel kids, Jimmy Lee and Bonnie.

"You're not getting any money if you help," said Lars, "so if that's your idea, forget it."

"I don't care. I'd rather help clean out a barn than stay around home all day."

Mamma agreed that Marie could go with Lars and help. Marie knew Lars didn't protest because cleaning a barn full of manure and putting down straw was nothing anybody could enjoy and an extra worker, even Marie, would help him and Homer get the job done quicker.

Homer was busy shoveling manure out of the cow stalls when Marie and Lars arrived at the Byers's barn. Lars picked up a shovel and began helping him.

"You go up in the haymow, Marie, and start pitching down straw," Lars ordered.

The haymow was full of straw and Marie was used to doing this relatively easy job. She'd pitched down straw at home plenty of times for Alfred and she didn't mind doing it. She thought about how Trudy said Henry was a bootlegger and that he had moonshine booze hidden under the straw in his barn and that was the real reason he didn't want any livestock. She'd told Marie not to tell because if people knew what Henry was doing, he could even go to jail. As Marie pitched down the straw, she wondered if now that Trudy had broken up with Henry, she was still held to the promise not to tell about what old Henry was doing. She'd like to make some trouble for him; but no, that would mean trouble for Max and Myrtle too and it wasn't their fault Henry was such a jerk.

"What the hell are you two doing in this barn?"

Marie heard Henry Byers shouting! Her hands froze on the pitchfork in terror as Marie realized what Lars and Homer would not know. Henry could act crazy when he was that mad. Trudy had told her he carried a gun, a pistol, with him wherever he went. They might all be in danger.

"We're cleaning the barn!" Lars yelled. "What's it look like?"

"Both of you! Get out of here if you know what's good for you!"

Henry was drunk! He was acting crazy again and Marie thought about digging into the straw and covering herself up. Henry was swearing at Lars and Homer in a loud, mean voice. Lars was yelling too but she couldn't hear all he was saying to Henry. She didn't have any trouble hearing Henry. "I don't give a damn what the old man told you to do. I don't want kids in this barn!"

"We're not leaving without Marie! She's pitching down straw from the haymow," yelled Lars.

"Come down here, Marie!" bellowed Henry. Now she could see his fat, angry face glaring up at her from the opening by the haymow ladder. Marie was terrified.

"No!" Marie screamed.

"Then I'm coming up after you!"

Marie screamed louder. Her screams sounded terrible to her own ears. "Lars! Homer! Help me! Don't let him get me!"

Henry was mounting the ladder. Marie tried to climb the high pile of straw but she kept falling back. He would hit her! Hurt her! Henry might try to kill her! She screamed again and again. He was up in the haymow now, coming toward her! Marie kept screaming for help.

"Shut up! Shut your damn mouth, Marie!"

Marie was crawling in the straw now. She couldn't get up. She couldn't get away! He would get her! Marie screamed. "Help! Help! He's going to hurt me!"

What happened next went so fast, Marie hardly knew what was going on. As Henry reached out his big hand to grab her ankle, he fell, flailing in the straw. Homer Merkel had tackled him. Henry swore and managed to grab Homer by his hair, stagger to his feet, and then he threw the boy to the concrete floor below which was covered with the straw Marie had pitched down.

Henry fell. This time, Marie realized, it was Lars who tackled Henry. Lars pounded the big man with his fists before Henry could push him off and get up. Lars was on his feet swiftly and again he tackled Henry and he fell with a thud. "Think you're tough, huh," yelled Lars. "You can't fight fair so take this!"

Sitting up in the straw, Marie watched Lars kick Henry hard with his heavy work boot. Henry bellowed loud cries of pain as Lars kept kicking him.

"You want to fight dirty? See if you can get up and try to throw me!" Lars yelled as he kicked Henry repeatedly. Henry's howls of pain were deafening.

Marie climbed down out of the haymow. She'd have to hurry and get Max who was in the field or Myrtle who was in the house. Homer was lying very still on the floor. Maybe Henry had thrown him so hard he'd killed him!

Getting Myrtle would be quickest. Marie ran toward the

house, but Henry's sister was already coming out of the house and down the back steps. She must have heard the yelling.

"What's going on, Marie! What's happening out there?"

"Henry's here! He's acting crazy! He threw Homer out of the haymow and now he's trying to hurt Lars!"

"Oh, my heavenly stars," cried Myrtle Byers.

If everything wasn't so awful, it would have been funny to see plump Myrtle Byers take off running toward the barn. Marie entered the barn behind Myrtle and they saw Lars kneeling beside Homer. Myrtle quickly knelt down by Homer and cried, "Homer, speak to us. Are you hurt badly?"

"I don't know," said Homer. "I feel kind of funny. Just got the wind knocked out of me maybe."

"Where's Henry?" Myrtle demanded.

"Still in the haymow," said Lars.

"Henry! Henry! You come down here and quick!"

Marie didn't know Myrtle Byers could ever yell so loud and mean. She remembered, however, hearing Alfred telling somebody once about how tough Myrtle was when she was in eighth grade. He said she'd beat up any boy who dared to touch her baby brother Henry.

Big Henry Byers came clumsily down the haymow ladder, straw and chaff stuck to his body. He was moaning and blubbering, almost crying.

"Myrtle, I didn't do nuthin' except tell him to go down. He must've fell. If he's hurt, it's an accident. I swear to God, Myrtle, I never touched the kid."

"He's lying," cried Marie. "I was up in the haymow when he did it. I saw him grab Homer's hair and throw him hard as he could out of the haymow. Myrtle, Henry was trying to hurt me and Homer came up to help me. That's why he threw Homer out of the haymow!"

"You fool, Henry! You drunken brute!" yelled Myrtle.

Myrtle was still kneeling beside Homer. "You'll be all right, Homer," she said quietly now. "I think you were just stunned but I'm going to call a doctor to make sure."

"Myrtle, I never did what Marie said. They'll all lie to you. I swear I never even touched him," Henry whimpered.

Myrtle stood up and took a few menacing steps toward Henry. "Get!" she yelled and raised her hand as if to strike him.

Henry was cowering and crying now. A big man crying just like a little kid! Crying because Lars had hurt him and because he was afraid Myrtle might hit him. Trudy was right about Henry. He was a big coward and scared to death! Scared of a woman! Afraid of his sister Myrtle!

"They want more money, Myrtle. They're after me. You and Pa have to help me or I don't have a chance. They're big time and they don't fool around. They told me if anybody finds out what we've been doing, the sheriff will be looking for us and before that they'll come looking for me. Myrtle, I'm your brother! Pa's turned against me. You have to help me!"

"You get out of here, Henry," Myrtle screamed. "Haven't you hurt father and me enough? You came here last night and demanded money from your own father at the point of a gun! He gave it to you and told you not to come back! So I'm telling you—*get!* If you don't, I'll have the law on you, Henry, even if you are my brother!"

"Please, Myrtle, I'm beggin' you."

Marie saw Myrtle hesitate for a minute, look from Homer lying on the floor and then back at Henry. Myrtle stepped closer to Henry until their faces were only about a foot apart. Then Myrtle said in a cold, even voice, "Get, Henry! I said get!"

Henry ran out of the barn. Then Myrtle Byers picked Homer up in her big strong arms and carried him toward the house. Marie and Lars followed. Marie noticed Henry just sitting in his blue Buick parked at the short driveway entrance. Marie and Lars went into the house behind Myrtle and Homer.

Suddenly a shot rang out and Myrtle screamed, *"Oh, God, no!"* She was still carrying Homer in her arms, and the two little Merkel kids, Jimmy Lee and Bonnie, could be heard crying upstairs in the room Myrtle had made into a nursery.

Henry's high school graduation picture was in the Spencer *News Herald*. It said that Henry Byers, 31, prominent Clay County farmer had died of a self-inflicted gunshot wound. The newspaper account said his mother was deceased and his survivors were his father, Max, and his sister, Myrtle.

Marie read the account of Henry Byers's death twice and looked at his picture. He didn't look bad when he was younger. He wasn't so fat. It made her feel strange. She was there when it happened! When Henry Byers killed himself! Why had he done it? She remembered the day at the lake with Trudy when she'd almost drowned. How afraid she'd been that she'd die so young! Why did Henry do it? Was Henry so afraid to live that he'd rather be dead?

Alfred, Lars, Mamma, Cora, and Milton went to Henry

Byers's funeral. Mamma said Marie should stay home with Karen. Marie was glad she didn't have to go. It was all so awful. While Karen wrote a letter to Rosie telling her about Henry, Marie went down and sat on the pighouse. She was fourteen now, too old to climb up on this roof as she had done ever since she was a little kid; but she could think here and she had to think. She didn't like feeling the way she felt about Henry! She felt so mixed up!

Marie couldn't cry about Henry but she didn't hate him anymore. There was no longer any reason for that. He was dead. She looked out across the rows of tall green corn and remembered the last lines of the Longfellow poem that she'd spoken so often here on the pighouse roof:

> Thus alone can we attain
> To those turrets, where the eye
> Sees the world as one vast plain,
> And one boundless reach of sky.

Why was it that she hadn't been able to remember the middle of the poem but she'd remembered and said the end? Maybe it was because the end was the most important part. Maybe it was like what Reverend Norgaard had told them about memorizing all the things he made them learn in confirmation class . . . "You must first learn the words and the meanings I have taught you . . . the memory of the word of God will remain in your mind and much later when you are older you will understand that what I have taught you is knowledge to preserve your faith, your faith in God Almighty!"

Marie looked out across the fields of tall green corn to

the "one boundless reach of sky" and still couldn't understand why Henry had done what he did. Why had he killed himself? She'd been there when it happened. Myrtle had put Homer on a couch, and then she'd run to Henry's car with Lars and Marie. Henry was slumped over on the seat and his head was covered with blood. Lars had run to the field to get Max and Myrtle had called the doctor but it was too late.

Marie climbed down from the pighouse roof. There were times you couldn't bear to look at the bright blue of the sky and this was one of those times.

A few days after Henry's funeral, Trudy Horton came out to the Carlsen farm with her mother. Only Marie and Mrs. Carlsen were home. Alfred and Lars were in the fields and Karen had gone to play with one of her neighborhood friends. Erma Horton sat down at the kitchen table and drank coffee with Mamma, but Trudy went with Marie up to her bedroom. They sat on Marie's cot bed, and when Marie looked directly at Trudy's face she saw tears in her eyes.

"I keep thinking about Henry, Marie," she said. "It makes me feel so bad. We went to his funeral, Ma and me, and out to Max and Myrtle's house to eat afterward. It was so sad. There were a lot of people at the funeral and at the house too. But Marie, I didn't see any friend of Henry's there. They were all neighbors and people from Max and Myrtle's church. There weren't any other relatives. Henry didn't have anybody related to him except his father and sister."

"I know," said Marie, "Mamma said Mrs. Byers died when Henry was nine. I never knew of the Byerses having any cousins or aunts or anything."

"That's what was so sad," said Trudy. "Henry didn't have any friends either. None of the people that Henry hung around with came to his funeral. They didn't care anything about him except as a bootlegger. That's what was so sad about Henry's life, he didn't have one special friend. Not even me! The only reason I ever went out with Henry was because he bought me things and took me places. And Marie, I wasn't a bit nice to him when I broke up with him," Trudy said, wiping tears from her eyes with a handkerchief.

"Trudy, nobody liked Henry so don't feel bad. He made everybody hate him because of the way he acted. You know that," said Marie, hoping to comfort Trudy.

"I guess that's true," said Trudy, "but that's what's so sad. He hurt people, but Marie, don't you understand? Henry hurt himself most of all. You see, Henry didn't even like himself! That's why he killed himself. He wasn't special to anybody, not even to himself . . . and Marie, that's what's so sad. I never knew Henry to be really happy. . . ."

It wasn't long after that talk that Trudy decided to transfer to cook in a hotel in Des Moines. The people who owned the hotel where Trudy worked in Spencer owned a much larger hotel in Des Moines and had told Trudy she could go to night school if she worked in the capital city. Trudy said she could have a room in the hotel and eat all her meals there, go to school at night until she got a diploma, and maybe she'd really have a chance now to make something of herself. She called on the telephone to say good-bye before she left on the bus. "Don't worry, you won't get rid of me. I'll come out to see you guys when I come home to visit Ma and Jake."

A letter came from Magnus from Denmark. He was working in Copenhagen and he said it was easy for him to find a job because he could speak and write English as well as Danish. It was good to be back home in Denmark but conditions in Europe were getting worse. Hitler was becoming more powerful in Germany and there was no telling what he was planning to do. Magnus was worried but he said he was glad to be home again, close to his family. Marie worried about Rosie. No letters ever came from her and it was almost August.

18

Long Distance Call after Midnight

IN HER DREAM MARIE KEPT HEARING THE SOUND. OVER and over she heard the ringing sound. Then she woke up. It was no dream. It was the telephone. Two shorts and a long. Two shorts and a long. It was the Carlsen telephone ring on the party line.

But it was the middle of the night. Still dark in the room! Marie jumped out of bed and ran downstairs as the telephone stopped ringing. Mamma had answered it. She was in her nightgown and her long graying dark hair hung down her back.

"No," she said. "No, it can't be. It cannot be Rose!"

Marie listened. Her heart seemed to stand still. Something had happened to Rosie! In the dim light that came from a living-room lamp, Marie saw the stricken look on Mamma's face as she listened to what she was being told.

144

"Yes. Yes." Then, "yes it is my daughter Rose. She does have a birthmark as you mention on her back. It is Rose. Oh, dear God, it is my little girl!"

Mamma was crying now. Marie heard her tell whoever was on the phone to send the body to Cobb's Funeral Home in Spencer. Mamma hung up the receiver and turned from the phone.

"Rose was killed in Illinois," she said to them for Alfred and Lars, barefoot, were now up too. "That was a sheriff from Elgin on the phone. She was on a motorcycle with Nick who was badly hurt. He gave them my name to call."

There was no more sleep for anyone except Karen that night. Alfred called Cora in Everly, Trudy in Des Moines, Uncle Jens in California, Cousin Dagmar in Chicago, and Tante Karen who would tell others.

It rained the day of Rosie's funeral. It was a warm late August rain but it brought some relief from the heat. The funeral was small. Trudy came home from Des Moines on the Greyhound bus, otherwise mourners came from no long distance.

After the funeral service, family, friends, and neighbors stood at the graveside and listened to Reverend Norgaard say a few last prayers for the departed soul of Rose Anna Carlsen Kravensky. When it was over Mamma walked falteringly between Cora and Myrtle Byers who held her arm. Katie Tornquist held Karen's hand. Marie stood alone, crying, until Lyle Tornquist came over to her and put his arm around her.

Rosie was buried beside Papa. It was what she would

have wanted Mamma said because she had been so close to him. Marie looked at the green grass that covered Papa's grave and the dark mud of the one that had been dug for her sister. Lyle stood with her as she cried.

Marie was not prepared for the way Rosie's death made her feel. At first it had been a numbness, a disbelief, then anger at everyone including herself. Nothing mattered now that Rosie was gone and would never come home.

"I'm not going to high school," she told Mamma one day. "It doesn't matter whether I go or not. I'd rather just stay home and work around here."

'No, you must go on to high school, Marie," said Mamma. "Someday you must make your own life away from this farm. You must learn more in order to prepare for that life wherever it may be."

"What good did it do Rosie to go to high school?" Marie asked, knowing that she was being cruel to Mamma but not caring because her own hurt was so deep. "All she ever did was work in a stupid laundry and do a lot of dumb jobs that anybody could do without going to high school."

"Rose enjoyed high school. She had many friends and they enjoyed her. It was a good time in her life. I want you to listen to me, Marie, and then you may decide for yourself whether or not you want to quit school."

Marie did not want to listen to a sermon. She was afraid Mamma would tell her a Bible story, like the preacher, and try in some way to make it apply to Rosie's life. Marie was sitting at the kitchen table and Mamma poured herself a cup of coffee and sat down at the table with Marie.

146

"Let us talk about grief, Marie," she said. "It is part of life and only those who cannot think escape it. You think deeper than most so perhaps you will suffer more grief than others. You are much like your sister Rosie."

It was the first time Mrs. Carlsen had called her daughter "Rosie." The word had a strange sound from her Danish-accented tongue. It was as if she were relating to the dead girl through Marie's mind instead of her own.

"Let me tell you of eleven-year-old Rosie for you do not remember her, Marie. Your father gave her that name when she was two days old. 'She has a face like a small rosebud. Let us call her Rose,' he said. So soon she became Rosie to everyone, even your father, but to me she was always small Rose. We were so happy with our little boy Alfred and two sweet little girls. We decided to build a big house and fill it with children. We have spoken of joy, Marie. Now let us speak of grief."

Mamma did not look sad or old or tired. She seemed strange. She put a large strong sunbrowned hand over Marie's thin long fingered hand which lay on the kitchen tablecloth. She squeezed Marie's hand and the touch was warm.

"As our little Rose grew, our family grew. She grew in a quick and sunny way and I knew that she was her father's favorite. She tagged after him to the fields, always bright and chattering. How he loved her. It was, I think, a special kind of understanding they had for one another. I lost a baby girl after Lars. I have never spoken of her because it was what is called a miscarriage and it seemed best to forget. She went nameless to the grave. Then two years later you were born, Marie. What joy you brought us. 'Another Rose face, but let us call this one Marie after your mother,' he said. Three years later there was Karen. When she was two months old, Papa died."

Marie listened intently. She had never known that there might have been a sister between her and Lars. It made Mamma seem almost a stranger as did this talk of Papa who had lived in a world that Mamma remembered and she did not because it was buried in the past.

"She came to me, my small eleven-year-old Rose, tears streaming down her face and asked me why. 'Why did God take Papa from me? I want him back.' And I could not comfort her. But there was one who could. Her name was Marie. Rose was the one who took this small Marie into the fields to help her herd the cows or pull the weeds."

"I don't remember that," said Marie.

"Of course you do not. What does a three year old remember of sorrow? But it was you, funny chatterbox that you were, who drove the tears from Rosie's eyes and brought back the smile to her face."

Mamma took away the hand that covered Marie's. She took something from her pocket and laid it on the tablecloth in front of Marie. It was Rosie's high school graduation watch.

"I think Rose would want you to have this, Marie. She was a girl who always knew the time. Sometimes, I suppose, she wanted to move time back or move time forward. But *now* is what is important. *Now* must not be wasted. Think about what I have told you. Then decide if Rosie would want you to waste your time being sad, going around with a long face, when there is so much to learn of the world she loved and had to leave so young."

Mamma said she had to pump water for the chickens. She left Marie sitting at the kitchen table. Rosie's watch lay on the table. It had been in a package that was sent to the funeral home with Rosie's body. Marie did not want the watch. It had probably been on Rosie's arm when she was killed.

She picked it up and put it to her ear. It was ticking. She checked the time with the electric kitchen clock on the wall. It was the right time. Somebody had set and wound the watch, probably Mamma.

Marie put the white gold wristwatch in her pocket. She would keep it but she'd never wear it. She remembered once she had taken the watch from Rosie's dresser and worn it to school to show Joyce and Irma Henderson. Rosie had been really mad at her and said, "I thought it was lost and I looked high and low for it. Keep your mitts off my watch, Marie. If you break it, I'll never get another one."

Marie went upstairs to the bathroom. Trudy had gone back to Des Moines. Karen was spending a few days with Cora and Milton in Everly before school started in September. Lars and Alfred were helping neighbors thresh oats. Marie looked out the bathroom window and wondered how the world could continue in its usual manner, so unchanged, even though Rosie was dead and buried and no longer one of the living.

From the bathroom window she saw Mamma open the barnyard gate and close it behind her. She watched her walk beyond the pasture toward the cornfields. Marie went into the big front bedroom that had once been Cora and Karen's, but was now just Karen's, and lay down on the bed. She lay on top of the pink chenille bedspread that Cousin Dagmar

149

had sent Mamma from Chicago so long ago. Memories of Rosie and Nick flooded her mind. Then she cried. Alone in the house on a hot August afternoon, she cried until she felt empty of tears, exhausted, and sleep came as it does finally to a lost and frightened abandoned child.

When she awoke the house was quiet and empty. She took the watch out of her pocket and checked the time. It was almost six. She had slept two hours.

She heard the horses and the clattering sound of the hayrack coming up the driveway. Lars and Alfred were home from eating supper at the place where the day's threshing had been done. Marie looked out the south living-room window and watched the hayrack and horses come to a sudden stop near the barn.

Lars at eighteen was over six feet, slightly taller than Alfred. The ten years difference in their ages was no longer so obvious. They worked together, unharnessing the horses and leading them to the watering tank.

Marie saw Mamma coming from the pasture. She stopped at the tank for a moment, talking to Lars and Alfred. Then she unlatched the barnyard gate, came through it, closed it behind her and walked toward the house.

In her hands were two ears of yellow corn. Marie knew what she had been doing. She had been walking through the corn rows, checking the kernels for hardness, signs of maturity, and readiness for picking.

"It is a good crop," she told Alfred and Lars that night. "I found many ears ready to pick. These two will be good for seed. We must start saving the best for next spring's seed corn. The worms have not hurt the harvest. Yes, it is a good crop." Mamma seemed so strange.

150

Alfred and Lars went to bed early because they would have to be up early and go threshing the next day. Marie went up to her bedroom. She tried to sleep. She felt so tired but when sleep came it was fitful and she kept waking up and crying.

She knew now that this room, Rosie's old bedroom, could never be her room. No matter what she did, paint the walls, change the furniture, and take every reminder away like Rosie's curtains, the ghost of Rosie's life on the farm would always be in the little room by the bathroom.

She'd never be able to forget Rosie moving over on the cot to make room for her and cuddle close to her warming her cold body. "Can I sleep the rest of the night with you, Rosie? It's so dark and I'm cold." And she remembered her big sister's sleepy voice and how her pillow smelled like Yankee Clover cologne. "Okay, get in quick," Rosie would say pulling her close to her warm flannel nightgown. "Kiddo, you're cold as ice! Turn around and bend your knees. I'll make you a chair and we'll keep each other warm." Remembering was awful now! Marie buried her face in the pillow and cried herself to sleep.

❧ 19 ❧

How Alfred Feels

MARIE WAS AWAKENED BY A KNOCK ON HER BEDROOM door. She thought it might be Mamma but when she turned her head, it was Alfred who had opened the door and stood looking down at her. Her first thought was how awful her brother looked, almost like a tramp.

"You better get up, Marie," he said as he walked into Rosie's bedroom and looked out the west window. "The sun's been up for a long time. It's almost ten o'clock."

"I didn't sleep very good last night," said Marie. "I kept waking up and thinking about Rosie and wondering where Nick and the baby are. Why doesn't anybody know what happened to them, Alfred?"

"Nick was hurt pretty bad from what they told us. They took him to a hospital in a little town in Illinois. Nobody knows why, but somehow in the night he managed to put his clothes on and leave the hospital. He was gone in the morning and there wasn't a trace of him. It was almost as if he wanted to get away and hide . . . or hide something. Maybe he was afraid somebody would take his baby. Maybe somebody did. . . ."

"He was Rosie's baby too," Marie said, trying to hold back tears. "Nick didn't have any right not to tell us where he was. Now we'll never get to see him."

"Marie, there are people checking things out. It's hard and it may take quite awhile. Rosie and Nick were farm laborers who moved from place to place wherever they could find work. It's pretty hard for officials to trace people who can't settle down in one place long enough to have neighbors and make friends."

"I don't care," said Marie. "They should have come home and then nothing would have happened to Rosie. Nick didn't have to take Rosie and the baby all those places."

Alfred turned from the window and looked at Marie. His eyes were red and he needed a shave. Alfred's face looked old and tired. There were lines on his forehead and around his mouth that she had never noticed before. Alfred had changed since he left home. He had changed even more since Rosie was killed. Alfred didn't look young and handsome anymore. He looked old and tired and he was only twenty-eight.

"Marie, it's Ma I'm worried about now," said Alfred. "She's given up. When I think how much she's changed. How all the fight and spirit have gone out of her . . . I don't know what to do, what to say to her. I look out the window and see the big buildings like the barn and the granary that she was so proud of because they were built to last for generations of Carlsens . . . and I wonder . . . what's the use? Is there any use in building things when nothing lasts. . . ."

"Is Mamma sick?"

"I don't know," said Alfred. "It's kind of the way she was when Pa died. She's kind of gone back into her own head in a strange way. She acts like she accepts whatever happens as God's will or something. But she's different. I can't talk to her. Neither can Lars. It's like there's somebody there who's Ma but she's not Ma anymore."

Marie understood what Alfred meant. All the bossiness had gone out of Mamma. It was like the way she was when she told her she could decide for herself whether or not she wanted to go to high school. It was like she didn't care what anybody decided to do anymore. Marie felt afraid thinking about the conversation she'd had about high school and Rosie and Papa when he died when Marie was three. It was like what Alfred was saying now . . . Mamma seeming different and strange.

"The thing that worries me about Ma," said Alfred now, "is the way she feels about Karen."

"Karen's still with Cora and Milton in Everly," said Marie, "so what do you mean, Alfred?"

"She wants to just leave her with them. Karen doesn't want to come back home to live and Ma says that's Karen's decision to make. She says she won't make Karen come back here to live unless that's what she wants to do. That's not Ma talking. Giving up Karen is the last thing I ever thought Ma would do."

Marie sat up in bed. Then something *was* wrong with

Mamma! She had given up being the one who gave orders, told people what they had to do, and tried to be in charge of everything. What did it mean . . . *that Mamma didn't want to be Mamma anymore?*

"When Pa died, Ma let Tante Karen take you and Karen home with her before the funeral. You were three and Karen was a baby. She didn't show any interest in having the two of you come back home. She acted real strange and said Tante Karen might as well keep the two of you as she was better able to take care of you. Finally, Cora and I just got in the car and drove to Tante Karen and Uncle Soren's farm and brought you kids back home where you belonged. After that, Ma started being her old self and started making decisions again. Marie, it really worries me. Ma's acting the same way she did when Pa died only this time I think it might be worse."

Alfred was looking out the west window again. After awhile, he looked back at Marie.

"This farm was always her security. You see, she made a promise to Pa before he died that we'd all grow up together here on this farm, in this house that he built for his family. But she was afraid she couldn't do it. She didn't even think she could live without him. That's why she let you and Karen stay with Tante Karen. But finally she got over his death because she had a family to raise and a farm to manage. She had a purpose in life and a promise to keep to Pa. She thought if she could keep the farm and always have a secure place for us to live that we'd be safe."

"And that's true," said Marie, "if Rosie hadn't gone away with Nick, she wouldn't have been killed."

"No, Marie," said Alfred. "We don't know that. She could

have been killed right here at home in an accident or died in some other way. It's what Henry did that makes Ma doubt everything she ever believed in. Henry shot himself. He was too afraid of life or whoever or whatever threatened to hurt him or send him to jail. Ma told me that Max blames himself for Henry's suicide. Max told Ma that he'd kept Henry a boy instead of making him get out and learn to live on his own without any help. It's so ironic. Rosie left home because of hard times and now she's dead. Henry never had the guts to do anything except stay around here and get mixed up with some two-bit bootleggers who had him scared to death most of the time. How do you figure it? I don't know, Marie. I just know Ma can't turn Karen over to Cora. That's crazy."

Yes, and it was crazy for Karen to think she could live with Cora and Milton in Everly. It was even crazier for Mamma to say it was up to Karen to make the decision of where she wanted to live. Yet in a way Marie understood. Karen had always been close to their big sister Cora. When Mamma was busy working outdoors in the garden or tending the animals, it had been Cora who took care of Karen and Rosie who had looked after Marie. When Rosie went away, Marie had moved her things into Rosie's room and Karen had stopped sleeping with Mamma and began sharing a room with Cora.

Marie remembered now. After Cora and Milton were married, Karen had asked Marie to share the big double bed in the front bedroom with her. Marie had refused, saying she liked having her own room. After Rosie was killed, Karen had gone back to sleeping with Mamma downstairs. Afraid to sleep alone, Karen who had never been afraid of lightning, cats that scratched, cows that kicked, or even afraid to put her hand under an old hen that pecked when she gathered eggs in the henhouse. Karen had always been much braver than Marie. But now Karen was afraid. Afraid of growing up. Marie didn't think she could explain this to Alfred. He probably wouldn't understand that Karen had reached the age of being afraid of staying a baby and being afraid of growing up. Marie understood this feeling. She'd had it herself when she was Karen's age. Yes, and she still had that feeling now. She might as well admit it (at least to herself). She was afraid of having to grow up and also afraid of never growing up. When, she wondered, did a person ever get over feeling that way. Did Alfred sometimes feel like that? She couldn't ask him. He probably wouldn't want to answer a question like that, especially now that he was going on thirty.

"Marie, what I really came up here to talk about is you. I want you to go to high school. Ma said she was going to leave that decision up to you. That's not Ma talking either. You could decide something now that could hurt you later. I want you to go to high school, Marie."

Marie turned her face away from Alfred. She knew tears were beginning to fill her eyes and she didn't want Alfred to see her cry. She didn't want him to feel any sadder than he already did. How could she explain to Alfred why she didn't want to go to high school, that going away from home (even if it was just into Spencer to a big school) meant she'd grow up and have to learn to work some place other than at home . . . *and she was afraid.* She couldn't tell Alfred that she was afraid of having to grow up and leave home!

"Why did you tell Ma you had decided not to go to high school, Marie?"

"I don't know," said Marie, not looking at Alfred because

she was afraid she might cry when she had to tell the truth. "I guess because I'm afraid of having to grow up and leave home. I mean like Rosie and. . . ."

"Okay, I can understand how you'd feel that way. When Pa died it was October and I was a junior in high school and Cora had just started as a freshman. I was almost seventeen and Cora was fourteen, the same as you, Marie. We both quit school because our lives had changed so much. After Christmas that year, Ma decided we both had to go back to high school because Pa's death, she said, couldn't change the fact that we both needed more education. Well, both Cora and Rosie did graduate from high school, Marie, but I never did. Ma couldn't talk me into going back to school."

"Why wouldn't you go, Alfred," asked Marie now because she had always wondered why he had quit and her sisters had not.

"Ma always thought it was because I was too stubborn," said Alfred, "but it wasn't that. I was afraid, Marie. Maybe I felt the same way you do now, afraid to go out in the world on my own, feeling safer here at home. I don't know why I didn't have the guts to go back. I always liked school . . . learning things. All I know is, it was a mistake to quit high school. Ma always had hired men. I didn't have to quit. She wanted me to finish and I could have if I'd had the guts. It was hard for me to go through the electrician trade school course. Sometimes I was afraid I might not pass. I found out I wasn't near as smart as I thought I was. Sometimes I'd have to stay up all night doing assignments that other guys could do in a few hours."

"But you did graduate and you are an electrician now,"

said Marie, hoping to help Alfred feel better about himself.

"Yes," said Alfred, "and I owe that to Ma. She was the one who came up with the money and really made the decision that I should leave home and learn a trade. If she was herself now, Marie, she wouldn't leave the decision up to you. She'd make you go to high school. I can't tell you what to do, Marie. It's got to be your choice now. Just think about it before you make a wrong decision. I know a lot of farm girls never go beyond eighth grade, but Pa always wanted all of us to graduate from high school and even go on to the university if we were smart enough. You're smart, Marie, so think things over. That's all I ask."

"All right, Alfred," said Marie but she was still afraid of leaving home some day. Going to high school and having to grow up would be so hard, so much harder than she had ever imagined. Alfred smiled at her now and turned away. She heard his footsteps on the stairs as he went back down to the kitchen. Marie could visualize Mamma sitting at the kitchen table, drinking black coffee, doing nothing, acting strange. Poor Alfred. Poor Mamma! Marie got out of bed and started getting dressed. Maybe she could talk to Mamma. Somebody had to!

20

Karen

KAREN STAYED WITH CORA AND MILTON FOR OVER A week. She didn't want to come home.

"That's sure strange," said Lars. "She's always afraid I'll forget to feed her cats. She never wanted to be gone at night before, not even when she was with you, Ma."

"It is not so strange," said Mamma. "Karen is suffering grief also. Don't think because she is still so young, that she has not suffered the loss of her sister. It will take some time and much love from all of us for her to accept what has happened to Rose."

"But when are Cora and Milton bringing her home?" Marie asked.

Marie thought Mamma looked sadder and older than she had in the two weeks since Rosie's funeral. "They can't bring her home," said Mamma. "She will not get into Milton's car. She told them she's not coming back here to live. Not ever." And Mamma looked like she might cry.

Marie went to her mother and put her arms around her. This was too much! Even for Mamma. Why did Karen have to behave like this and make things so hard for Mamma? Then she remembered her own cruel remarks and her insistence that she was not going to go to high school. How stupid! Of course she had to go to high school. What could she ever do if she didn't? And of course Karen would have to come back home to live and go to school. It was impossible for her to live in Everly with Cora and Milton. Karen was afraid, Marie knew that.

Really it was just as stupid for Karen to think she could always live in Everly with Cora and Milton as it was for her, Marie, to think she could hide herself away at home and never face going to high school and someday leaving Mamma and everyone at home. What Karen was doing, the way she was acting, was different and yet it was somehow the same Marie reasoned.

Karen wasn't behaving in such a stubborn way because she was stupid because she wasn't stupid! Karen had always been bright. Then she remembered what Mamma had said to her at the kitchen table when she had given her Rosie's high school graduation watch . . . "Let us talk about grief, Marie. It is part of life and only those who cannot think escape it. You think deeper than most so perhaps you will suffer more grief than others. You are much like your sister Rosie."

Yes, Karen was bright and she cared so much about the things she loved like her kittens, and people she liked. Karen had cried when she learned that Magnus had left for Denmark and when Trudy went to Des Moines. Karen was bright and sensitive and Marie knew something else that maybe Cora and Mamma wouldn't know about. Karen didn't want to come back home and be faced with the reality of all the reminders of Rosie who'd loved both Marie and Karen so much! Marie knew how Karen felt now. Coming back home would mean having to start growing up, learning to do hard things, and trying to let go of longing thoughts of a time and life that were gone and could never be shared again. Marie understood how Karen felt and now her sadness was for Karen, not just herself.

"Don't worry, Mamma," Marie said now. "Karen will come home. After supper and after the chores are done tonight, we'd better all drive over to Everly and get her. I mean all of us—you and me, Alfred and Lars. She's still so sad, Mamma, she can't think very well. But when she sees how much we all want her to come back home, she'll come. Don't worry, Mamma. Down deep I know she wants to be here with you."

"All right, Marie," said Mamma. "We can go after her tonight. Poor baby. I just don't know what we can say to help her through this sad time. We'll just have to pray that we can help her understand." Mamma poured herself another cup of black coffee and Marie saw the tears coming to her eyes.

Marie went upstairs. She went into the room that Karen had shared with Cora and then into the one she'd shared with Rosie.

Suddenly the idea came to Marie. She worked very quickly. She carried her clothes, dresses, coats, blouses, everything on hangers, emptied all the dresser drawers, took all her books and even the bookcase, and moved all her possessions from the little room by the bathroom to the big airy bedroom in the front of the house.

From now on this would be their room, hers and Karen's. Maybe Mamma would like to move her bed upstairs now to Rosie's old room and use the downstairs bedroom for a sewing room or a spare bedroom if they ever had overnight company. Anyway, Marie thought she'd talk to Mamma about making some changes like that. If Trudy came home from Des Moines, on a weekend or something, it would be nice to have an unused extra bedroom.

Just as Marie had suggested, the whole family drove over to Everly to bring Karen home. For a little while they stood around in the kitchen and talked to Cora and Milton about Karen who had gone to the Everly grade school grounds to swing. Marie knew where it was and she went to find Karen.

She wasn't swinging. Karen was just sitting in one of the swings, pushing her feet back and forth on the ground. Marie hoped she wasn't crying. She wasn't.

Marie was the one who started to cry. "You have to come home, Karen," she said. "I moved into your room and I don't want to sleep alone. Why don't you want to come home and be with me? I hate being the only sister left at home."

Karen did what she always did when somebody cried and felt terrible. She showed that she felt sorry. Karen got out of the swing and put her arms around the sobbing Marie. "Don't cry, Marie. It's okay. I have to come home anyway. All my clothes and stuff are still there. I don't even have any clean underwear or socks at Cora's house. Besides, I don't think they'd let me go to school in Everly because I belong to another township. Anyway that's what Cora and Milton said. They don't even act like they want me to stay here so I'm going home with everybody tonight. Cora said she talked to Mamma and everybody wanted me to come back home and that the whole family was coming after me. Did they? I mean did everybody come along?"

"Yes," said Marie, "Mamma and me, Alfred and Lars, we all came and we all need you to come home."

When they went into Cora and Milton's house, Karen went straight to Mamma's chair and Mamma held her in her arms and stroked her hair. Mamma was smiling through her tears. That night Karen did not sleep downstairs with Mamma. She slept with Marie. "The house is starting to get cold at night," said Marie. "Turn around and bend your knees and I'll make you a chair," and Karen went to sleep with Marie's arm around her, knees tucked up snugly behind her. Marie was almost sleeping soundly too when Mrs. Carlsen opened the bedroom door, pulled the covers more closely up to their chins, stood looking at them in the moonlight for a moment, and then went downstairs.

❧ 21 ❧

Without the Scar

THE MORNING OF THE FIRST DAY OF HIGH SCHOOL IN town, Marie changed her clothes six times. It was so important to wear the right thing and not look like a farm girl. She finally decided upon her brown wool skirt and brown and orange twin sweater set.

She'd been brushing her hair a hundred strokes every night and it did shine even if she didn't like the way the metal curlers left it refusing to be combed the way she wanted. She wished she could have had naturally curly hair like Rosie.

Rosie. Oh God, she was dead! What did Marie care how she looked? Looks didn't matter that much. But how about the town kids? What would they think of her the first day of high school? She'd read somewhere that first impressions were important.

Marie heard the sound of a car coming into the driveway

and a horn honked several times. There wasn't time to worry about how she looked. She ran downstairs, picked up her new high school books and brown paper sack lunch, and ran to George Knight's 1926 Hupmobile. Lars was already in the back seat and Homer Merkel was in front with the Knight boys. The boys ignored her except to say such things as "shut the door, Marie," or "open the window, will ya?"

Marie was not prepared for the fear she felt as she entered freshman English, her first class. There were almost twenty strangers in the class. She didn't know anybody. The town kids knew each other, having gone to school together for many years. They ignored her. Marie felt completely cut off from the laughter, greetings, and jokes, which did not include her. She was glad when the bell rang and the teacher insisted upon silence. She wondered if she would ever have a friend in this school of strangers.

At noon she went into the high school gym where the rural kids ate their sack lunches. Town kids went home at noon. The farm girls sat together and the farm boys did not mix with them. The country girls were friendly and different from town girls. But Marie sensed that, like herself, they felt inferior and shabby because they would never be included in the inner circle of town girls' activities. None of them, for example, would ever be elected to student council, become president or secretary of a club, or be invited to join the town girls for a soda at the drugstore after school. Farm kids had to go where their cars were parked and go home right after school and do chores. Marie understood now why some farm girls had liked living in town even though they had to work for room and board.

166

"My name's Maxine Humphreys. What's yours?" asked a plump girl with red hair who was eating her lunch next to Marie.

"Marie Carlsen."

"Is this your freshman year?" asked the girl. "I'm a sophomore. I transferred from Emmetsburg."

The girl was wearing an ugly green crepe dress that looked like it had been made over from a woman's dress. She had warts on her pudgy hands and dirt under her fingernails. It was obvious that she was looking for a friend and Marie seemed a likely prospect. Talking to Maxine Humphreys did not lessen Marie's sense of loneliness. If anything, it doubled it!

One day followed another and soon Marie knew her way around the almost five-hundred-pupil high school in Spencer. Still she hated to enter a classroom alone to which other students went in pairs or groups. She'd never belong! She was too shy, too awkward, and nobody would ever think of her as anything but a dumb farm girl.

It was a completely miserable feeling, sitting in the Hupmobile after school, all alone, waiting for the neighborhood boys and Lars to come to the car and drive to their rural homes. Maybe she'd quit school! But she couldn't. Mamma would never want her to do that! But how could she stand four years of such unbearable loneliness?

A red-haired boy with freckles approached the car. Oh God, it was Red Gillette! He was a friend of Homer Merkel's and had something he wanted to tell him. He'd wait for him in the car. Oh dear God, she was alone with Red Gillette, the best-looking, most popular farm boy in the sophomore class! She remembered how he'd helped her pick up cobs and told her he liked her after she beat him in the foot races at the township picnic. It was different now! She felt awkward and tongue-tied alone with him. She couldn't talk to boys anymore!

"You're Marie Carlsen, aren't you?"

"Yes," Marie said, knowing perfectly well he knew who she was.

"Remember the time you beat me in a foot race?"

"Yes."

"Bet you couldn't do it again! I went out for track last year. I got a letter. Did you know that?"

"No."

"Well, I did. Made up my mind nobody was ever going to beat me running again. I went to the Drake Relays in Des Moines last year. Did you know that?"

"No." Marie had not spoken to Red Gillette since the night of the box social when he'd shown his preference for Angeline Carter. She had purposely avoided him. He seemed to have forgotten his bad manners that long ago night and Marie didn't feel like reminding him. Red Gillette laughed. "Sure don't talk much, do you? You going to the fair this year?"

"Maybe. I don't know yet," Marie said. Oh God, why didn't Homer or Lars or somebody come back to the car so she wouldn't have to talk to Red? Why couldn't she think of something funny or smart to say to him? Why did she have to be so shy and bashful around boys?

"I'm going," said Red. "I've got a calf. He might win a blue ribbon. It's an Angus bull. If I win, I'll go to Sioux City."

"Oh," said Marie.

With relief she saw that Lars, Homer, and Darrell were approaching the car from the Rexall Drug Store. Thank God! Now Red Gillette would talk to them while they waited for George Knight to stop talking to his town girlfriend and come to the car.

She had a dream one night that was so real it seemed to be true until she woke up. She was happy in the dream. In the dream she looked like Rosie and she was wearing a red skirt and a white angora sweater. She was laughing and saying all sorts of clever things. Sitting on the edge of a desk in the study hall, she was the center of attention. Red Gillette, the track star, and four or five of the most popular town boys in school surrounded her, hanging on her every word. In the dream she was pretty, popular, and terribly witty! She was exactly the way the rich town girls seemed to be. She woke up. The real Marie—bashful, dull, and plain looking, went to school with Lars and the neighborhood farm boys in the Hupmobile.

She came home from school one night and Karen was running down the driveway to meet her and Lars when they were left off on the shoulder of Highway 71. Karen's face was wreathed in smiles. She was now in sixth grade and taller than Marie. Blond and pretty, Karen was a delight to everyone who knew her.

"Guess what?" she cried. "We got a letter today and it was about Nick and the baby. It's from a Mrs. Hamilton. She's old and can't keep him and she wants somebody to go to Chicago and get him. He's two years old!"

The address on the letter was 7720 Green Street, Chicago,

Illinois. Karen said Alfred knew where it was, not too far from cousin Dagmar's house, and he was going after the baby Friday night when Cora didn't have to work and could go with him to hold the baby coming back home. Marie was so excited, she was afraid she might wet her pants. Thanks, God, thanks, God. Oh, thank you, God, she kept saying to herself as she ran to the house. Rosie's baby had been found and he was going to be theirs!

At first Mamma said she was too young to take care of a baby all the way home from Chicago. Then she said it was Wednesday and Marie couldn't miss two days of school. But Alfred was so anxious to leave that he talked Mamma into letting Marie be the one to go to Chicago with him to get Rosie's baby.

It was a long trip to Chicago in the old Essex. Alfred put three extra tires in the trunk just in case they had some flats and they started off that night for Chicago. As they drove down Highway 71, past Storm Lake, and on toward Des Moines, Marie felt it was like a dream. Too good to be true. But it was real. She was on her way to Chicago with Alfred to get Rosie's baby!

They drove all night. Marie slept in the back seat. Once she woke up and saw a million lights. It was Des Moines Alfred said and after midnight. She went back to sleep and when she woke up again they were in Illinois. It looked just like Iowa, miles of cornfields and little towns along the highway. All day they drove through Illinois and it was almost dusk when they reached Chicago.

Marie stared with wonder-filled eyes at the factories, the rows of houses, the crowded streets, as Chicago stretched for what seemed fifty miles. Finally there were the towering skyscrapers, a glimpse of Lake Michigan, and the street Alfred was looking for, Halsted, the longest street in the world he told Marie.

"I know that Green Street is right off Halsted. If I stay on Halsted, I can find seventy-seven twenty Green," said Alfred.

They drove for miles where there was nothing but black people. They had their own stores and schools but Marie knew they were poor. Poorer than any people she'd ever seen. The children had no nice places to play and washing hung from upper story clotheslines that stretched from one tenement building to another. How awful, Marie thought, how awful to be so poor and live in Chicago where you could probably never go to the country where the air smelled nice and there was plenty of room for kids to play.

When they reached the address Alfred was looking for on Green Street, Marie's stomach felt like it was going to flop over. It wasn't from hunger. Alfred had stopped and they'd each had a hamburger and milkshake. It was excitement, but Marie did not feel like she'd throw up. She felt like she used to on Christmas or on her birthday before she opened a big present!

The woman who opened the door when they knocked was not Mrs. Harold Hamilton. She was the landlady. She sent them upstairs through a hall covered with boldly flowered wallpaper to a room with a sign on the door. The sign said two words, "Madam Zelda."

A small, old woman with a wrinkled face answered their knock. She beamed when Alfred told them who they were.

"I can believe you are Rose Anna's sister," she said. "You are the image of my Nicky's wife. How beautiful! How sweet your face. Come, let me show you our precious one."

And precious he was. His hair was yellow and curly. He had the sharpest blue eyes Marie had ever seen. No, that wasn't true. She had seen such blue eyes once before. Nick's eyes! He looked exactly like Nick. Only without the scar.

Marie picked him up out of the crib in which he stood, and held him in her arms. He was not a heavy baby, but rather small and thin for a two year old. Marie was now as tall as Rosie had been, maybe a little taller. The baby looked at Marie, a long intent look, and then he said, "Mommy."

"No, I'm not your mommy. I'm your Aunt Marie," but the baby said the word again, "Mommy."

Madam Zelda said it had been more than three months since Nick and Rosie had left the baby with her. "He sees the resemblance, poor little one," she said. "At such a tender age, he does not remember perfectly. How he cried when they left him to work in the fields, harvesting vegetables. They could not take a baby with them. After awhile, he was content with me. But he remembers. Yes, he is a smart one. He remembers his mother even though this one has too young a face. She has the same smell, the same touch, and she is beautiful. Yes, the child remembers the essence of his beautiful mother."

It was a strange feeling that the baby should think she was Rosie. Rosie, whom he would never see again. It was a good feeling, a warm feeling, that made Marie feel closer to God than she ever had in church. It was proof that she had grown up to look and act like Rosie. Or that some part of

172

Rosie still lived. Marie wanted to cry or laugh. She didn't know which. She looked at Alfred. There were tears in his eyes.

Madam Zelda told them all she could about Nick and Rosie. They'd come to her when she was working with the Royal American Shows at a fair in Missouri. The baby was little. They had moved from town to town, working at whatever jobs were available for any of them. Taking turns caring for the baby, living in rooming houses, hotels, or migratory workers farm shacks.

"It was hard," said Madam Zelda. "But we were together, a family. There was much love between my Nicky and Rose Anna. He lived only a few days after they told him his Rose Anna was dead. He had lost the power to use his hands but he dictated a letter to his nurse. That letter told me that he wanted you, Rose Anna's people, to have their baby. He knew his old Aunt Zelda was too old to bring up a child and he did not want him to grow up in an orphan's home. He did not want that kind of sorrow for his son."

"Thank you. Thank you, Aunt Zelda, for giving him to us," said Marie.

"I did not give him to you, sweet Marie," smiled Aunt Zelda. "Rosie and Nicky gave him to the world and God gave him to himself."

Madam Zelda packed a small suitcase with things that had belonged to Nick and Rosie, clothes for the baby, and a strange looking old Bible. It was something like Papa's Danish Bible except it was written in Polish. On the cover was a name in gold—Jacob Nicholas Kravensky.

"You will take good care of this book please," said Madam

Zelda, "and see that he gets it when he is a man. It belonged to my brother, Nicky's grandfather."

Before they left, Madam Zelda took Marie's palm and read her fortune. She read her life line. "There has been much sorrow in your life," she said. "Yet to come will be much happiness. I see bright lights and music, a boy who runs swift as the wind, a boy who loves animals and the land. I think you know in your heart which boy I mean."

Red Gillette! My God, it couldn't be anybody but Red Gillette. If she really was pretty and looked like Rosie, maybe he wanted her to go with him to the fair. Bright lights and music. That had to be the carnival!

"Do you really believe the fortunes you tell," she asked Madam Zelda.

"I am Catholic and we believe only God knows life's secrets," the old lady smiled, "but in each life there is hope and that is the only kind of fortune I read."

"But how about Nick and Rosie? They didn't have any hope, did they?"

"Oh, my dear, those two were filled with hope. It fairly bubbled from them when they were together. They are together now. When you look at a sunset or the stars you will know they are together some place so bright and dazzling that human tears cannot exist."

It was early evening when Alfred, Marie, and Jacob Thomas Nicholas Kravensky drove into the evergreen-lined driveway from Highway 71. The September sun was brilliant behind the huge farm buildings that could be seen from the highway. As they parked the Essex by the pump deck in the backyard,

Marie could see the pighouse roof between the trees of the grove, which were shedding September leaves. The sun was even more glorious behind that low roof because you could see more of its brightness. The whole family, even Cora and Milton were anxiously awaiting the first sight of Rosie's baby. Marie didn't mind relinquishing him to his grandmother's arms as everyone clustered around the old Essex. It had been a hard job taking care of a two-year-old baby all the way from Chicago. Certainly a job that no child could have done. Marie carried the suitcase into the house.

"Marie, guess who called and wanted to talk to you this afternoon," said Karen. "Red Gillette! He wanted to know if you'd come home from Chicago yet."

"What did he want?"

"He asked if I thought you'd go with him to the fair next week."

"What did you tell him?"

"I said I didn't know, maybe."

Suddenly they heard the phone ringing insistently. It was the Carlsen party line ring. Karen ran to answer it. "It's Red Gillette, Marie! He wants to talk to you!"

"Tell him I'm busy. I just got home from Chicago. Tell him to call me tomorrow or maybe I'll see him in school."

"Marie, he wants you to go to the fair with him!"

"Okay," said Marie. "I might. I don't know yet."

Marie was not at all sure now that she had the chance that she would really want to go to the fair with Red Gillette. After all, when you've been to Chicago, it's hard to get excited about going to a county fair with somebody who's never been any place bigger than Des Moines or Sioux City.

She remembered that Lyle Tornquist had once gone to the fair in St. Louis, but the thing that had impressed him most was the airport there. She decided to call Lyle and tell him all about her trip to Chicago and to tell Katie to come out and see Rosie's baby. Marie talked to Katie first and then to Lyle. He had no interest in Chicago. He had something to tell her!

"*I flew, Marie!* While you were gone, I went to the airport and the manager took me up in a plane. He even let me take the stick and fly it myself for awhile. *Marie, I flew!* You can see everything . . . the fields, the towns, the roads and cars, even rivers. The buildings and cars look like toys from the sky. Marie, flying is the greatest thing in the world!"

Marie didn't tell Lyle but she was sure she'd never have the nerve to go up in an airplane. She didn't tell him about Chicago. Oh well, when you stopped to think about it, there was nothing so great about Chicago. It was just a lot of buildings crowded together . . . like Spencer, Sioux City, or Des Moines . . . only bigger! Much, much bigger! Bigger, but empty somehow, now that Tommy was no longer there. Maybe someday Marie would go back. For now, she'd stay here, where the old house was full of memories and of new life and new beginnings. And where the autumn sunsets blazed beyond the pighouse roof.

Instructional Materials Center
C. W. Post Campus Libraries
Long Island University
Greenvale, NY 11548